THE MORTICIAN

JOHN BARACKMAN

Edited by Jacob Floyd

Edited by Paula Nevins of Ember & Ink Author Services.

Cover design by Christy Aldridge of Grim Poppy Design

Formatted by Megan Nevins of Ember & Ink Author Services

PROLOGUE

It was the backcountry of Middle Tennessee, in the year of Our Lord nineteen hundred and twenty-one. While it may be acceptable in the big cities like that of Nashville, this was, after all, the "Roaring Twenties," where Tin Lizzies spouted their noxious tailpipe fumes, and speakeasies dotted the back alleyways down by the loading docks, where men and women mingled together and drank the Devil water, all the while dancing like the blasphemous sinners they were. And where the city women wore dresses with hemlines all the way up to knee height, exposing ankle and calf for any man to gawk at—but the deeper truth was, in this here backcountry of the great Hog 'n Hominy State, horse and buggy was the norm. Here, sober men and women praised God every night and went to church every Sunday. They worked the land by day and attended to their families by night. The soft lights of candle and oil lamp illuminated the living rooms of these good country folk, and not the harsh light of the electric bulb like those folks in the cities did.

But for one such God-fearing countryman, who somewhere between the shadowy crevices of the Tennessee River Valley, and the deep recesses that lay in every man's soul, he lost his way in this here life.

On one very beautiful, warm day, it had all begun; in the deep green landscape of a graveyard made lush by the hot and humid air of summer in the South,, a mortician by the name of Horace, was hard at work digging a grave.

Beside Horace was a casket. And in that casket lay a dead woman; bled to death from the struggle of childbirth—tragic though this may be—it was an all-too-common way for a young woman to go in those backward times. As Horace dug this poor woman's final resting place, behind him a few hundred paces back, by the old Oak tree that had stood a hundred years in its spot towards the North end of the graveyard, two strangers walked from seemingly out of nowhere, out onto the peaceful grass between the many headstones that dotted this part of the cemetery. A tall man in a black suit and a Woman dressed in sheer silk scarves had come to watch this lone mortician at work. They were not from the physical plane of the planet Earth, however, as she was an angel and he a demon. Had Horace not been so busy with his task at hand to look up and behind him, he would have seen only two wisps of fog in the grass of his cemetery plot, so gossamer were their visages. But, it should be that neither did Horace see the other spectral beings, those of the undead, that restlessly walked these grounds as well. The Angel looked to the Demon and said, "There may be time to save this one; he has yet to cross the dark line."

The Demon looked to the Angel and replied with a dark gravel voice, "Not as of yet, but I feel this one will be lost to this world; you shall see my beautiful one, you shall see. I predict his fate is a baleful one and he shall soon reveal his true identity."

It was at this very moment that Horace finished his digging, pulled himself out of the grave, and walked over to the head of the casket. He looked this way and that to be sure he was alone, that no one was lurking about the graveyard to spy on what he was about to do. He quietly opened the casket cover. The dead woman was, before her untimely death, still in the tender blush of youth, had not yet turned green from the rot of death. Horace gulped and slid his hand down her dress to cup her right breast. Her breast was cold and hard, but he felt his manhood stiffen nonetheless as he pinched her nipple.

The demon looked across to the Angel and chuckled with a deep, sonorous laugh that sounded like the scrape of a knife against a sharpening stone before returning his horrible gaze to Horace.

Sadly, the Angel, saying nothing, simply turned and walked away, disappearing as she had come through the curtain between the worlds and onto the other side.

I
THE CREMATORIUM

Horace Graves walked on the Franklin Pike as he headed back from the town of Columbia towards Springdale, Tennessee, his place of birth and current residence, after a much-needed visit to the local Piggly Wiggly grocery store. *Not much of a road, really,* reflected Horace regarding the Columbia Pike, *just a hard pack set of tracks in the dirt so a horse 'n buggy can make their way along.* He walked slowly, not wanting to get too sweaty, for the summer heat had begun to rear its hot, humid character over the lush greenness of his hometown after the relative coolness of that spring. And due to his birth infirmities, he stepped with a limp.

Being a mortician by trade, he dressed in a stiffly starched suit and coat, with his tie pulled tight to his collar. Although stifling hot, Horace would never consider dressing otherwise. *After all,* he reasoned, *this bein' the proper and dapper way of the mortician.*

He carried in his arms two large cloth bags of groceries, which loaded him down and slowed his gait. *I will enjoy this supper tonight,* he thought as he trudged forward, sweat dripping from his forehead, *only one more mile to go...*

As Horace approached the knoll where the Franklin Pike

crested the Allisona Hillocks that overlooked the valley his property lay in, he reflected on the green of the countryside he called home. The beauty of his surroundings would sometimes nudge Horace out of his typically puckish mood; Horace was *almost* happy. *At least there are a few things in life worth living for,* he thought forlornly as his eyes scanned the lush greenery common to the South.

Horace looked along the spine of the hill the road stood atop. Down at the base of the valley, where the river at the base met the ridge just northwest of him, was his property, not a mile away as the crow flew. He could see the southwestern corner of his property line where his humble and modestly profitable pig farm lay. At this distance, the pigs he owned were small dots of pink to his eyes. They were milling about in the yard, enjoying the warm morning sun.

Above the pig farm, just at the edge of his vision at the crest of the rise, were the cemetery grounds.

"The Graves Memorial Park," pronounced Horace out loud as he squinted at the rays of sunlight that glinted off the polished marble of the gravestones.

His family had owned the graveyard for three generations, first purchased as an abandoned church with its small cemetery plot by his paternal grandpappy, Percy Graves. *More* 'n *four score years of grave diggers by God!* declared Horace to himself.

Horace had made it to the base of the rise leading to downtown Springdale. What remained of Springdale was that. Horace looked left at the dilapidated remains of a building that had been Mrs. Cornwall's boarding house in the old days. Now only rats, crows, vultures, and the occasional drunk'n stumblebum called it home. Just down the road was the ruin of the general store. Boarded-up windows, holes rotted through the wood stoop, the J.R. Gibbs General Store est. 1810 sign lay broken off to the side. A rusted-for-sale sign probably hung at the entry to the store and forgotten since the mid-1880s, still swung in the wind. The rusted hanger hooks made a loud *squeak* when the wind blew.

Horace's shoulders dropped at the abject loneliness of his town. Although there were still plenty of country folk living in the woods around these parts, as far as this town was concerned, he was the sole town member now.

BACK IN 1880, when Horace's father, Franklin, was nineteen years of age, the ruination of the Civil War was long gone, and the Gilded Age of the Industrial Revolution had shifted into full gear. Being at the nexus of river and railroad, Nashville was at the center of this revolution for the nation. Nashville was bursting at the seams with newly minted manufacturing companies.

Company representatives, desperate to fill their factories with workers, scoured the landscape over hill and dale, pasted advertisements for employment in every small town that dotted the landscape for a hundred miles around the Nashville town center:

Jungermann & Co., Makers of Fine Confections, Looking for experienced bakers!

W. H. Perry Brass Foundry & Machine Works needs YOU!

Apply Now To: L.L.B. Shaetz, Manufacturer of Shirts, Stetson Hats, and Fine Neckwear!

Morton J.W., Maker of artificial limbs, needs experienced machinists. Apply Now!

Posters for boiler makers, broom and brush manufacturers, cigar importers, "Gentleman's Outfitters," whiskey distillers, paper makers, and so on and on and on and on, littered every public billboard and post big enough to staple to. Posters over posters. Posters blowing in the wind and littering the landscape. People collected these posters and burned them in the fireplace for heat.

So, the good God-fearing country folk of Springdale packed up and moved to where the money was: Nashville.

Springdale drained of its population, like a stopper pulled from a sink full of water.

In the fall of 1885, not long after his father, Franklin Graves, wed his sweetheart, Elizabeth Grebe, Horace was born. Elizabeth, after a long and difficult delivery, bled to death two days after the delivery. Franklin did not call a doctor. He and Horace's grandmother, Annebel Graves, whom they called Granny Graves, did their best to save Elizabeth, but the birth had gone grievously wrong. He didn't have money for a doctor, as mortuary customers were rare in those days, nor were there doctors to be found; they too, had fled to Nashville. Franklin Graves simply cleaned up the bloody mess, embalmed his wife, all the while tears streaming down his face, and buried her next to Percy Graves, Horace's paternal Grandfather. *Thank God I have my mother to lean on,* thought Franklin.

As Franklin looked upon his newborn son, he knew life would not be easy for his child. He was obviously deformed. He looked sickly. Thin and stooped. Too long a nose. The boy was born hairy—thick wads of gray-black hair grew on his back and his head. Gray pallor. And to add to this strangeness, his son did not seem to cry. Ever. A thought briefly entered his mind: *It might be best for all if'n I take him out back and shoot him,* but he dismissed this as ungodly.

"He looks like a vulture!" he exclaimed to Granny Graves in shock.

"Hush now, Franklin," replied Granny Graves, "This be only a baby, an' innocent of all things evil."

Mayhap thought Franklin ominously as he looked down at his son. *Mayhap.*

ON HORACE'S TENTH BIRTHDAY, rather than throw Horace a birthday party, Franklin began his new "Special Project" instead. A few days prior, Franklin had returned from the Morticians Convention and Exposition of 1895 held in downtown Nashville, energized by something he had seen on display. It was the talk of the convention. Franklin pulled out the plans he had purchased from the brother of the inventor and current patent holder: Carl Heinrich von Siemens. Franklin jabbered on and on to Horace about how he would build this fancy "newfangled device!" to "cleanly" dispose of the dead. A device called "a crematorium."

As Franklin explained the workings of this device to his son, Horace imagined being pushed headfirst into a small coffin-like room, the flames turned on, then screaming in pain as the flames slowly burnt him to death.

"No, no, no, my son," comforted Franklin, "the people you put in the crematorium are already dead—they burn to ash, then you sweep up the ashes with a broom, put the ash in a little box, and hand the box back to their loved ones."

This did not comfort Horace as he looked askance at the crematorium plans. Morticians at the convention trumpeted cremation as a more sanitary means of disposing of human remains than that of burial, (*no noxious effluvium to contaminate the groundwater!*), But Franklin saw things from a different angle. He believed the process would catch on with the many members of the Evangelical Revivalist movement that was sweeping the Springdale area and thereabouts. Franklin saw it as a way to boost his sagging business. *Those German 'n*

Czechoslovakian immigrants that fill the Evangelical prayer tents every Sunday like the idea of being spiritually cleansed by fire... Moldering in their grave smacks of impurity to 'em. Throw'd in low cost with those pinchpennies an' it be an easy sale! Franklin thought with excitement.

So, Franklin built his crematorium using firebrick and steel obtained from the foundries in Nashville, bought mostly through side deals for little or nothing—trading the coffins he made for the materials he needed. By the end of 1895, his crematorium was fully operational.

He changed the sign out front, adding his new service to the existing sign, which now read: *Graves Mortuary, Crematorium, and Memorial Park.*

After a few visits to the local proselytizing services of the Cumberland Presbyterian Church to hand out business cards and press the flesh, the business did indeed pick up. Some. Enough to keep food on the dinner plate, that was.

SIX YEARS LATER, in 1901, Horace was sixteen. His education in mortuary science had begun with a bang.

A middle-aged woman who had died the night before from an aortic aneurysm, "She just a suddenly stood up like she'd go'nt to the store and then dropped dead right where she stood!" claimed her grieving widower. The widower, Mr. Jameson, delivered his dear dead wife to the *Graves Mortuary, Crematorium, and Memorial Park,* in the back of a horse-drawn wagon, a blanket covering her body. Her feet, still wearing the shoes she wore the night before, stuck out the bottom of the blanket.

Fifteen minutes after Franklin had calmed the widower, assuring him that his beloved wife, Malinda, would be in good hands, "First she be in *my* hands, then she be in thine hands of God."

Shortly after, Mr. Jameson had left to return home, Malinda was naked on Franklin's embalming table.

In his first lesson in preparaing a body for viewing, Horace assisted his father. He had never seen a naked woman before. His eyes were wide round orbs.

First, he watched his father embalm.

"...The dead must not rot before the viewin'. This embalmin' fluid keeps 'em pink an' smellin' fresh as flowers," said Franklin.

Then, Franklin showed him how to carefully place the eye covers over the eyeballs, lowering the eyelids over the small spikes on the eye cover to keep the eyes shut and looking natural.

"...So they don't sink in, or'n open unexpectedly to stare at the living!" explained Franklin.

Next came sewing the mouth shut.

"... O'derwise the mouth might pop open at the worst moment during viewing!" educated Franklin.

Lastly came sewing the anus and vagina closed.

"... This need be done, so dey don't make a mess in the viewin' chamber when their families are gathered round to say their goodbyes. That no one wants to smell."

Horace almost asked his father to wait a moment before sewing her vagina shut—he wanted more time to look around a bit—but then Horace thought better of asking his father this.

SIX YEARS after that first lesson, in the summer of 1907, Granny Graves died of consumption. It was a slow and painful death.

Franklin brought his mother into the mortuary and did all the things a mortician does to prepare the dead for the long winter of death.

"No way is my mother goin' to burn up in a glorified furnace! No Way! My mother will join God and the Angels as a whole human being! As beautiful an' youthful as I can make her!" Franklin was shaking in anger, pounding his fist onto the preparation table as he said this.

Horace watched as his father feverishly worked on his Granny Graves. Franklin even used his new "Miracle Embalming Fluid!" he had been working on to show off at the next mortuary conference. This fluid, being mostly alcohol, formaldehyde, pine tar, and beet juice to make it red, stank up the room as Franklin pumped it using a hand crank and a large needle stuck into the brachial artery of his Granny's arm. Horace held his nose.

"With this embalming fluid, ten years go by an' y'all dig 'er up, she be as fresh as daisies. Fresh as Sunshine 'n Rain," explained Franklin.

He continued, "Now, 'n addition, we'll use them rouge on 'er cheeks to make 'er look youthful, as if she be asleep."

It was a hot July day, and Horace was sweating. He was wearing a heavily starched suit and tie, like his father was. They buried Granny Graves in a simple pine box next to Percy and Elizabeth Graves. Horace looked on solemnly as his father patted the last of the dirt onto the grave. "Goodbye, Grand-mamma," said Horace before he turned and walked back to the house.

Neither of them shed a tear.

That evening, after a tub bath and change into night clothes, Horace was reading The Bible. This was the only book he had ever read. He was reading a passage from the Book of Deuteronomy:

And he shall besiege thee in all thy gates until thy high and fenced walls come down, in which thou dost trust, throughout all thy land; and he shall besiege thee in all thy gates throughout all thy land, which the LORD thy God has given thee. And thou shalt eat the fruit of thine own body, the flesh of thy sons and of thy daugh-

ters, which the LORD thy God has given thee, in the siege and in the straightness with which thine enemies shall distress thee. The man that is tender among you and very delicate, his eye shall be evil toward his brother and the wife of his bosom and toward the remnant of his children which he shall leave, so that he will not give to any of them of the flesh of his children whom he shall eat, because he shall have nothing left him in the siege and in the straightness with which thine enemies shall distress thee in all thy gates.

After finishing the passage, Horace thought, *I feel in great distress and delicate of mind after my Grand-mamma died! Must I be evil toward my brothers? Do I have to eat someone?* Horace pondered on this a moment before shutting his bible with a snap.

Horace placed it on his night table, then turned to his side and fell fast asleep.

In the middle of the night, Horace woke with a start. He bolted upright in his bed and looked directly into the floating apparition of his Granny Graves. There she was, plain as day, sitting on a small cloud, floating just above the dirt floor of his room, right smack in front of Horace. Before Horace could cry out, his Grand-mamma began to speak, surprising him into silence.

"Horace, ye not be innocent no more, ye be damned if ye stay at this place," said his dead grandmother, which to Horace sounded as if she was talking through a long tunnel, "Be ye WARNED, Horace! Leave this place by the morn come."

At that, the apparition of Granny Graves floated up and away to nothingness.

Horace screamed. Within moments, his father appeared at his door in rather a bad mood at waking so suddenly (and snoring loudly after more than a few snorts of brandy…)

After hearing of the appearance of Granny Graves by Horace, Franklin slapped him across the face. "Don't you be botherin' me with this claptrap, young Horace. Now go to sleep! Mother Graves on a Cloud... Hogwash!" yelled Franklin. His father angrily stomped down the hall back to his bed, grumbling as he went.

After an hour of trembling and crying, Horace finally managed to sleep. Then dream.

In his dream, he lived in a stone castle replete with a wooden drawbridge and a moat. A demon, dressed in the skin of his Grand-mamma, the visage of which hid his horrible demonic face, pounded at the gates of Horace's castle. He dreamed the demon had bright red eyes as if lit by flames, a long face, long bony fingers, and fingernails sharp as talons. The fingernails were black as coal and curled inward. An unspeakable horde of the demon's minions stood behind the demon, ready to storm the castle. Horace feared the horde would grab him with their ghastly claws and drag him screaming to the flames of Hell. Horace, besieged inside the castle walls, held the gate doors closed with all his might. "I will not leave my castle!" yelled Horace to the demon.

The demon chuckled with a deep resonating tone that reverberated off the stone walls.

"I will see you as time goes by, and by my Young Master Graves," said the demon as it slowly faded into the dark of the background, the glow of its red eyes remaining a moment longer.

"The man with the red eyes is watching me," mumbled Horace in his sleep.

At that, the nightmare began to fade, then it passed completely from his mind. Horace slept soundly throughout the remainder of the night.

Horace woke that morning to the dim memories of the night's events. *By God,* thought Horace, *it is the Devil that is thine, Enemy. I shall not abandon the Gates. This be my land.*

The days came and went, and Horace never did leave, having completely forgotten his Grand-mamma's ghostly admonishment.

In the five years between then and the summer of 1912, Horace's steady tutelage in the art and science of caring for the dead had paid off, and Horace had become an accomplished mortician. At twenty-seven years of age, he was the youngest in his trade in the State of Tennessee.

But then his father suddenly died. *A heart attack,* Horace supposed. His father was quietly chomping on his breakfast of corn mash when his head simply fell forward into the mash. *No more yelling; this house now be quiet for once,* Horace thought as he pulled his father's head from the breakfast bowl. He dragged Franklin to the couch and then laid him down on his side.

After staring at his father's body for over an hour, Horace got up to see to his final care. He did not apply his skills to his father, however. Franklin had abused Horace far too many times for Horace to care much about his father's passing. Horace simply dragged his father out to the crematorium, rolled him in, closed the heavily insulated door, and turned it on. And since no woman would have Horace (the young women about the local area rebuffed him sternly whenever he tried), other than the occasional visitor for his services, he was now utterly alone in the world. Horace sat in the living room —*My living room,* he corrected himself—and read from the bible for company.

As Horace walked past the ruin of the General Store in May of 1921, lugging his grocery bags and sweating with the exertion of his long walk from Columbia, he looked to his right to the empty bones of the Springdale Public School. A chain-link fence with a rusted Private Property – Keep Out! sign clipped to it stretched the entire border of the school property.

"The Gov'mint shore do have them some monies to put a fence all the way 'round like that!" scoffed Horace. Horace had been a student there for a brief period when he was a boy, but as he looked through the chain link fence, he remembered his last day at school as if it were yesterday:

The teasing was progressively getting worse and more intense as his time at the public school evolved. Eleven-year-old Horace, enjoying the mild weather of that spring day, was in the play yard quietly playing a game of pickup sticks by himself when he suddenly found himself surrounded by five of his schoolmates.

They taunted him with a chant, "Grave Robber! Grave Robber! Grave Robber!" The chant went round and round as the classmates shoved and poked at poor Horace.

Another tormentor, a girl just a year older than Horace yelled, "Ewwww! I bet he kisses the dead girls!"

A thrown rock struck him in the head, drawing blood. Everyone in the circle laughed.

The loud chanting, "Grave Robber! Grave Robber! Grave Robber!" began anew.

That was when the strong hands of his father grabbed him and yanked him from the circle of children.

"You don't need that place, Horace. The Bible be the only book you need," Franklin said with a scowl over his shoulder towards the school grounds as they walked home together.

It was the last public school for Horace.

HORACE TOOK a last look at what remained of the abandoned old schoolhouse and continued his walk home. As he touched down on the east side of the Duck River Bridge that led to the entry gate to his property, he looked left at the acreage situated to the west of him. There, standing in the middle of the hay field, was a man about a hundred yards away. He could see that the man was unusually tall. He was wearing a suit, jacket, tie, and a hat. *A very debonair outfit: so unusual for a farmer,* thought Horace.

Although too far for Horace to see much detail, he could see that he had a very elongated face and hands. The man's fingernails appeared uncut for months, inches long and curled inward.

The man's eyes, looking at Horace, appeared to glow red *—or was that the sun glinting off his face that caused that look?*

Horace gave the man a quick, polite nod, then thought, *Where'd I see that man before? He looks strangely familiar...*

As if reading Horace's mind, the strange man nodded back and said, "But I do remember you just fine... and I will be seeing you again soon, young Horace."

The man, his red eyes burning brightly, grinned an awful grin that sent chills down Horace's spine.

Trying not to appear too rattled, Horace rushed to enter his property, his feet walking as quickly as he was able to move them without breaking into an outright run.

Been a mighty long walk I just did. Mayhap I be seein' things... he thought as he slammed the gate closed behind him.

Horace retreated into his cemetery grounds. As he walked, he read aloud the names chiseled into the polished marble headstones, which helped to quell his heebie-jeebies:

"There be Mr. and Mrs. Wilkinson, and their son Jeremiah.

"Over there under that headstone lay Mary and Abel Grebe who died of the Spanish flu.

"Baby Byron an' hid tiny headstone be there.

"Those'in there grave here'in be the Buchholtz family: Nicholas, Ruthie, Fred, Marcy, John, and Richard."

And on he read as he made his way passed the pig pen, stopping on his way to say hello to his favorite pig he had named Patty, then onward towards the crematorium.

As he passed the brick and steel door at the front of the

crematorium, Horace remarked to himself, *lately I usin' this device more to smoke pig meat than to cremate the dead.*

This was true, though Horace still made a small income from its intended use, his smoked pig meats were popular with the locals. Though he made a modest income by this means, Horace would never admit to anyone that he cooked the meat they bought from him in the crematorium. *No Sir!*

Horace entered his home through the back door, placing his bags of groceries on the dinner table before walking to the living room. As Horace sat in his favorite rocker, he reflected, *I ain't had company in this room with me for more years than I can remember... since me Pappy was still with the livin'.*

After a bit, Horace picked up his bible and read quietly to himself. He continued to read for several hours before making his way back to the kitchen to make supper.

"I will enjoy me this meal," said Horace to the empty room, trying hard not to think about the man with the red eyes.

II
BOYS WILL BE BOYS

Horace had decided to attend the annual Morticians Convention and Exposition late one night while sipping hot chocolate by himself, he sat in his rocking chair in the living room. The postal carrier, making an infrequent stop at the mortuary—Horace rarely received nor sent mail—had left a parcel in his mailbox out the front entryway on Franklin Pike.

The postal carrier, Mr. Slack, who preferred the personal touch, liked to slide the mail under the door of his various clients. However, even though Horace had made polite company with Mr. Slack from time to time, Horace had the distinct impression that Mr. Slack did not care to engage in conversation with Horace, only greeting him with a perfunctory "Hello, Sir," or some such brushoff before returning to his horse to gallop away. It, quite honestly, hurt Horace's feelings, so Horace soon avoided contact with him, requesting Mr. Slack deposit his mail directly to his mailbox. Horace would leave any post he had to send in the mailbox, the red flag pulled up, mounted on a tree next to the entry to his property. Unknown to Horace was that Mr. Slack was quite relieved that he was no longer required to engage in conversation with the weird and disfigured Mr. Graves, who quite frankly creeped the hell out of him.

The single piece of mail Horace held in his hand was a glossy pamphlet advertising the upcoming Mortuary Convention and Exposition for 1921, held at the Hermitage Hotel in downtown Nashville, three weeks from that very day. The pamphlet read:

To the Funeral Director, Mr. Horace Graves,

You are hereby invited to attend our illustrious and wondrous event! Please register and make your travel arrangements as soon as possible. The registration application is attached. The honor of your company would be most appreciated.

Sincerely,

The Convention Committee.

The pamphlet included a detailed list of invited speakers who would be making an appearance at the convention, including the titles of their respective presentations such as: "Make her cheeks rosy, red! The art and magic of postmortem makeup," had caught his eye.

Photographs of the hotel accommodations, the luxuries of which were beyond anything Horace had ever seen, made Horace tremble with excitement. The hosted buffets with their piles of foodstuffs titillated him, and the descriptions of the "Gentleman's Entertainment, not but a few blocks away!" riveted Horace with its naughty possibilities.

Horace turned the glossy endorsement over and over in his diminutive hands, feeling its lustrous, gleaming surface, and looking at the beautiful grandeur of the hotel, thinking that perhaps... perhaps... he might make a friend or two. *God, I could use a friend,* he thought. *The attendees would,* after all, he reasoned, *be fellow distinguished morticians.*

Having made up his mind, Horace filled in the enclosed application in the best hand script he could muster. But because he had attended a mere one semester of public school, with the balance of his schooling conducted in a herky-jerky and fitful manner by his father, his finest script looked rather childish and scrawled. His spelling left something to be desired as well, but he did his best, referring to his Bible for examples of proper spelling when needed.

He placed the completed application, plus the two-hundred-dollar fee, in cash into the envelope provided.

Two hundred dollars? thought Horace, *who would have ever imagined these events would have such a cost.*

He licked the paste of the envelope flap, sealed it shut, then walked the hundred yards out to his mailbox. He deposited the letter inside, lifting the red flag to signal the postman. The next morning, when Horace returned to look, the flag was down and the letter gone. Horace clapped his hands in excitement and returned to his home with a newfound buoyancy to his step.

Each day, Horace would pace the distance to the mailbox, open the lid, see that it was empty, then plod back to his home with a grim look of impatience on his face. It felt to Horace an impossibly long two weeks that, finally, on day fourteen, his daily walk to the mailbox paid off.

And on that day, a letter lay inside—he had received a notice of acceptance to the event! Horace did a quick dance in the dirt of the Franklin Turnpike before returning home to make his travel arrangements.

The next morning, Horace walked the mile through the woods to his nearest neighbor, Mr. Popovic, to ask if he could hire him to transport himself and his baggage to and from the event on the horse and carriage that Mr. Popovic owned. After a bit of back and forth, Horace managed to negotiate the price of half a smoked pig for the ride (Mr. Popovic insisted it be Horace's finest and fattest pig)

The deal struck, Horace returned home to pack.

By THE END of the week, Horace was on his way to Nashville, a steamer trunk of clothes and sundries in tow. The steamer trunk and all the finer suits it contained were his grandfathers who was a head taller and sixty pounds heavier than Horace. Horace had to take in all the seams and tailor the sleeve and pant legs to fit his small frame.

Horace had done the tailoring himself, using his Grandmamma's Singer treadle sewing machine. Although his sewing skills were adequate, the style was horrendously out of fashion—but Horace had no way of recognizing this as the public *faux pas* that it was.

Horace arrived at the Morticians Convention and Exposition of 1921 with his mouth agape—the hustle-bustle of downtown Nashville coupled with the scale and splendor of the Hermitage Hotel, truly a modern skyscraper at ten stories tall, and occupying one whole city block, had simply dumbfounded Horace. The only other city that Horace had experienced, Columbia, was no match for this.

Horace's mouth remained open as he dragged his steamer trunk up the wide entry steps leading to the reception hall, his head swiveling on his neck, from one side of the great room to the other, as he took in the ornate marble and wood of the Italian and French Renaissance design. Horace marveled at the beauty of the polished terra-cotta tile floors, the detail of the gold-leaf inlay of the bas-relief panels, the size of the pediment doors and arched windows, the number and scale of the hall balustrades, and the gloriousness of the stained-glass ceiling. Horace imagined he was a wealthy Roman Caesar, and this was his palace.

Before Horace could scratch the floor, dragging his truck across it, a porter ran up to him yelling, "Sir! Sir! Please allow me to help you with your baggage!" who then quickly grabbed the trunk from his hand.

Together they walked the remaining steps across the lobby to the reception desk.

Horace checked in and attended the convention for the next two days. He enjoyed the sumptuous meals served in the Veranda Room, listening as he ate to the invited presenters, and clapping politely when they completed their presentations.

He particularly favored the exhibits in the Grand Ballroom. One such exhibition, manned by the illustrious Professor of Egyptology, Dr. Ingerson Schoefield, was about mummification. The Professor's thesis, illustrated with numerous diagrams and poster descriptions pinned to the exhibit wall, was on the possibility of improving the quality and durability of embalming using many of the same techniques employed by the ancient Egyptians.

The title of the thesis was, "Can we preserve a body for time in perpetuity?"

Horace had spent the better part of an hour quizzing the Professor on the various herbs, oils, distillates, and other preservation techniques employed. He took careful notes in a small notebook he kept in his pocket. Horace was not entirely clear why he held such fascination with the subject; perhaps his Father's enthusiasm for creating a superior embalming fluid that would keep his Granny Graves "fresh as sunshine and rain?"

Perhaps. But it was at base a need to know that drove Horace to press Dr. Schoefield for details.

It slowly became clear to Horace that the Professor was growing weary of this non-stop questioning (in fact, at this moment Dr. Schoefield was thinking, *I must find a way to extricate myself from this annoying and weird little man...*) so Horace finally said his goodbyes and left for his room for the evening.

That night, Horace dreamed of mummies; but instead of being the dead, shriveled things in the pictures that Dr. Schoefield had shown in his exhibition, they were alive—animated with pink flesh and eyes that moved and looked at Horace. Horace was back at Dr. Schoefield's booth in the exhibition hall. But instead of Dr. Schoefield, Horace had a very pleasant and stimulating conversation with a mummy regarding the nature of life and death: "Is it possible to be alive and dead at the same time?" The mummy answered that indeed one could be in both worlds; "In fact, this was a preferred way to be!" Horace felt a happy sense of knowing, even wisdom, from this most stimulating of conversations. He thanked the mummy for its time, profusely shaking the mummy's hand before departing.

Horace slept soundly for the remainder of the night.

THE NEXT AFTERNOON, while making the rounds in the Exhibition Hall, Horace met up with a group of three young morticians in training, all about his same age. Horace had rounded a corner, not minding where he was going, when his head smashed square into the chest of the largest man of the bunch, he being barely over five feet tall, and the man over six feet. Horace's head hit hard enough that he rebounded, causing him to fall backward to the floor. The three men laughed heartily at Horace's mishap. William, the man with whom Horace had run into, offered a hand up to Horace.

"I do apologize for my clumsiness," said Horace humbly.

"No harm, no foul, my diminutive friend!" replied William, "I'm used to the clumsy antics of the occasional goof bohunk about these parts!"

Horace, missing the insult completely, replied, "Well, it's always a pleasure to meet fellow morticians! I am Horace; nice to make y'r acquaintances..." nodding his head and holding his hand out to each man in turn.

The group of men continued to titter at Horace's obvious social shortcomings. They each gave a quick shake of the hand in return.

When it became his turn, William, not missing a beat with

this odd duck before him, took Horace's hand and shook it with exaggerated enthusiasm, and said in reply, "Well, it is so nice to meet a fellow mortician too, my dear Horace!

"I'm William; this is my associate, Walter," pointing to the man to his left, "... and this dorky bookworm over there is George," pointing to the man to his right. George pushed his glasses up his nose with his index finger.

Horace tipped his hat to each upon introduction.

"Holy shit man! Where does a fella find glad rags like you're wearing?" said Walter to Horace as he continued his snickering.

Horace, not sure how to react to this, said in reply, "This suit be my Grand-pappy's. I had to take it in a bit, be'n I be a bit smaller than 'I'm but it shore be a dapper mortician's suit don't you agree?"

Everyone, except Horace, laughed a hearty guffaw at that. Horace could only look in puzzlement, *Was it something I said?* then giving himself a quick once over to ensure that some bit of food from his morning breakfast or some such had not made an embarrassing stain on his clothing.

Nearly choking from his fits of laughter, William said to George, "Butt me, you bastard milquetoast!"

George replied, "I fucked your mother last weekend, you bleedin' hemorrhoid!" but handed a cigarette over to William with a smile.

Walter looked to Horace and said, "What kind of Bug-Eyed Betty would boff the likes of your gimp-ass?"

Horace, not understanding a thing Walter had just said, could only look back at him with a puzzled expression.

William, taking the reins of the conversation from Walter, redirected this to Horace: "Hey now, my good friend! The boys and I are planning to take a trip to a speakeasy this evening down dockside—care to come along with us? Could be a real humdinger of a time..."

Horace, never having been to a speakeasy in his life but

having a vague understanding that this could be an evening of fun and adventure with fellow morticians, dumbly nodded yes.

"Excellent idea, William!" said George, clapping Horace on the back, "our bohunk Horace here may yet dip his wick in one of 'em cheap quiffs that walk those docks—I'll bet they'll bonk any scurvy blaggard with a pulse!"

Everyone, except for Horace, of course, knee-slapped a hard laugh at that.

After the evening dinner reception had concluded and the last presenters had finished their talks, Horace joined his new friends for the adventure to the infamous bawdy saloons of the Nashville "Gentleman's Quarter" that was located in the lower Broadway district; where alcohol flowed despite prohibition and the prostitutes paid "sin taxes" to the authorities to keep the bars (and their legs) open for business.

Nothing in Horace's background or makeup could have prepared him for what he experienced that night.

THE FOUR MEN, Horace in tow, piled into a taxi—a shiny new and roomy 1921 Sheridan Touring sedan painted bright yellow and stationed just out front of the hotel. Horace had never been in a car before, and this sedan was the biggest car he had ever seen. The four of them, plus the driver, had plenty of legroom to spare. Horace spread out in his seat and gawked out the open car window at the tourists and sightseers bustling about the crowded streets of downtown Nashville.

The streetlights that lined every street, lit by gas from the Nashville Gas & Light Company, illuminated everything with a gentle red-gold glow, enthralling Horace.

William, sitting on the right side of the front row passenger seat, leaned forward and said to the driver, "Take us to the finest of saloons that Cherry Street has to offer, my good man!" He then handed him the amazingly generous tip of two silver dollars. The driver's eyes opened wide momentarily before snatching the coins from William's hand, making them disappear quickly into an interior pocket hidden in the lining of his coat.

"You and your gentlemen friends will want to go to the Southern Turf at the corner of Second an' North Cherry Street," replied the taxi driver with a big wink to William. A big wink as in: *Believe me, you really don't want to miss this joint... it will be worth your while if you know what I mean...*

With that, the driver grabbed the wheel and whacked the horn twice with his palm—*honk, honk!* He pushed in the clutch, slammed the stick into gear, and smashed down on the gas pedal, sending the taxi rocketing off. Horace, still leaning forward as he gawked at the street life outside his window, jolted sharply back into his seat, he almost lost his hat, grabbing it by the edge of the rim before it tumbled to the street. Horns honked in anger around, but the driver paid them no mind as he sped away to North Cherry Street.

When they reached the Southern Turf, Horace was once again wonderstruck by the scale and scope of the lower downtown Nashville nightlife. Horace had lived his entire life in the quiet of the country—he had never expected how loud and chaotic this honky-tonk district would be. His mouth lay agape as he swiveled his head from side to side to take it all in.

"Horace! You gauche idiot! Stop staring at everything and get out of the cab! We ain't got all night! The girls are lined up an' waitin' for us to eyeball their goods!" yelled George from the sidewalk.

Horace, startled from his trance, opened the taxi door and jumped out to follow his newfound companions into the speakeasy.

ONCE INSIDE, Horace was vibrating with excitement as he looked about the voluminous first floor of the saloon. Columns of white marble lined the side walls. Four life-sized sculpted marble angels, all female nudes, hovered twelve feet above the patrons, standing on ornate platforms on top of giant pilasters, one in each corner.

Horace, who imagined these angels watched and judged him, felt a tinge of guilt at being in this place of whoring and sinfulness. Bronze statues stood everywhere. No empty spots remained on the floor or a tabletop, while gold leaf decorated the many inlaid carvings along the upper wall surfaces. Large paintings from the Masters hung on every wall. A myriad of mahogany tables and chairs crowded the busy floor on which a hundred patrons gambled, drank, and ate; some so drunk they had passed out—their heads flat on the table and snoring loudly. Nobody bothered them.

Dozens of waiters and barmaids dashed, back and forth from the bar to the kitchen and back, their arms piled high with food and drink. A man at a piano was playing loudly and singing bawdy songs.

A large bar occupied the southern end of the room, crowded by a multitude of customers slamming shots of whiskey, talking to their buddies with animated gestures, guffawing, clapping backs, and calling to the barkeep, "… Another round of whiskey for me an' my friends here!"

Horace felt the impulse to cover his ears with his hands, the cacophony was so loud.

William, yanking Horace's arm and breaking him from his reverie, said, "Come, Horace. If you want your cherry popped, we need to go upstairs where the real tarts are."

Horace followed the gang as they led him to a door at the back of the room. The door was solid wood and obviously very heavy and strong. There was a small peephole, about one foot wide and six inches high, installed into the upper section of the door, just at head height; the cover to it snapped shut and locked from the inside.

William rapped on the peephole cover with his knuckles. The cover popped open, and a man, very large based on the size of his face, looked out in a not-very-welcoming manner and said gruffly, "What do you want?"

William leaned forward, a shiny gold coin in hand, and began to speak in a quiet voice to the man behind the door. Horace could not hear the exchange, but he saw William gesture toward the others in his group, nod his chin to indicate they wanted to go upstairs, and then hand the man the coin. Horace heard a heavy bolt lift, and the door opened inward.

The group, Horace forming the rear, piled through the open door. The moment Horace had cleared it and was on the inside landing, the door guard slammed the door shut and slid the large iron latch down, locking the door tight. Horace looked up at the door guard and gulped—he must have been the height of two heads taller and an equal measure wider than he. The door guard did not smile at Horace; he imagined the guard growling deeply like a bulldog about to bite. Horace turned quickly and ran up the stairs to catch up with his companions.

At the top of the stairs, Horace stepped through a curtain and into the room beyond.

"God Almighty above!" was all Horace managed to get out.

Like the floor below, the room Horace looked into occupied the entire span of the second floor of the building. As his eyes adjusted to the dimness of the room and began to focus on his surroundings, he saw a sight that he could not have imagined in his wildest wet dreams. The walls were entirely windowless and painted a deep shade of red. Thick velvet drapes of gold cloth, hung from the ceiling, hung in wide arches along the upper third of the walls. Between heavy marble balustrades spaced symmetrically around the periphery of the room were giant oil paintings of women, their ornate picture frames gilt in gold leaf. The women in the paintings, seated, standing, lying lazily on couches, were naked. The illustrated details of their female form were generous.

Horace let out a "God have mercy on my soul..." as his eyes drifted downward to the floor level. There he saw women in the flesh, seated, standing, and milling about, wearing little if anything in the way of clothing. All were bare-breasted. One woman, bouncing on the lap of a patron, was bare-naked. Server girls, wearing only thin see-through scarves around their waists, were walking about the aisles balancing trays of drinks. Other women in various stages of undress were chatting up the male patrons in the room. Horace let out, "Holy Mother of God..."

William, George, and Walter, having been watching Horace, let out howls of laughter.

"Come, my naive friend, put your tongue back in your mouth, and let's find us a table," said William with a slap to Horace's back.

Spying a group of men getting up to leave towards the back of the room, they made their way across the crowded floor to the newly vacated small round table, its four empty chairs beckoning to them. A server girl stopped to clear the table and take their order. Her long, curly, golden blond hair bounced most beautifully as she spoke. Horace noticed her perfectly round, pink nipples on her large breasts matched the color of her lipstick.

"We'll have us a round of whiskey, my sweet young thing," said George.

The girl pinched George's cheek and replied, "A round of whiskey coming right up."

The girl quickly returned with the drinks. "Will that be all?" she said with a wink.

George replied, "Perhaps a bit later, after we've quaffed a drink or two, you can come by with a couple of girls to entertain us?"

"Sure thing, sugar," she replied with an even bigger wink. She then immediately turned and left, her blond curls bouncing most appealingly as she walked.

George lifted his glass to toast, "Here's to beautiful blond-haired and pink-skinned women," and knocked his drink back in one gulp.

"To naked female flesh," followed Walter.

"May a beautiful whore scratch my back and bite my ear while I boff her tonight," added William, swallowing his whiskey down.

Horace, never having drunk hard liquor, sipped his instead. The way the whiskey burned his throat startled him. Coughing slightly, his voice hoarse, said, "Yes... an' to something much better than dead girls."

Suddenly aware of the silence, Horace looked up to see his companions all staring at him. Realizing what he had just said, Horace's face flushed a deep shade of red.

The others at the table burst out in fits of laughter. William started to choke, he was laughing so hard.

"Oh, Horace, tell me you don't fuck the dead ones," cried George, laughing so hard he could barely get the question out.

Horace began to splutter, "Well, no... of course not... Who would do such a thing?"

"My backward simpleton, there are morticians that engage in such things—believe me... And you bein' all gimpy an' butt ugly as you are, I wouldn't be surprised if you're one such poor slob," chuckled William.

Horace, stung by this rebuke, sat silent for a moment, staring into his drink.

He looked up to find a serving girl heading his way. He saw that she had a pretty body but a face that was not much to look at—a "Bug-Eyed Betty" as his table mates would no doubt have called her. Suddenly coming to the decision that he had to show these guys that he was a man after all, he reached over and grabbed her arm as she was about to pass. He said to her, "How about you and I have a go at it upstairs?" as he openly stared at her bare breasts.

"Ewwww! I think not, you creep!" came her immediate reply. She yanked her arm away from his grip and quickly dashed away.

He blanched with anger and embarrassment at this rebuff. Another round of uproarious laughter burst from around him, not just at his table, but from the occupants of the neighboring tables that had witnessed this as well.

"Oh my God, Horace. Even an ugly quiff won't have you. How do you live with yourself?" burst out Walter.

Horace could endure the humiliation no longer. He shot up from his seat and stomped to the exit. He heard George behind him cry out: "Here now, my man! You needn't leave—We'll find you someone who will let you dip your corn dog in 'er batter. We'll even offer 'er a blindfold!"

William clapped George on the shoulder, "You are such an ass, George." But on William's face was a broad smile.

More laughter, this time from the entire bar, erupted as Horace crashed down the stairs, out the door, and to the streets below.

TEARS welled in Horace's eyes as he marched the six lonely blocks back to his hotel with his hands buried deep into his coat pockets. His head hung low in shame. *Never again,* he promised himself, *will I allow myself to get close to people.*

They're not to be trusted. I don't need anyone. He burst out with a sob as he pushed on.

Heading into the hotel lobby, Horace, having pulled himself together somewhat—his eyes were puffy red, but he had managed to stop crying—decided to visit the small hotel drugstore for a quick drink of elixir to calm his nerves. He sat at the counter and ordered his paregoric from the soda jerk manning the fountains. As Horace sipped his elixir, he saw out the corner of his eye that a woman had sat down on the stool next to his. She was quietly looking directly at him.

The woman who sat before him was full-figured; she had a simple beauty that struck Horace as regal and elegant. She wore no makeup, yet there was not a blemish on her face; her features were soft and gentle. On her head, she wore a wreath of flowers, but she was unadorned otherwise. She wore colorful silk scarves around her, but her body underneath was naked and clearly visible through the scarves; nor was she wearing any shoes. Horace gulped.

"Horace," began the woman speaking softly, "You're not locked onto the path you have set for yourself. You still have time to change the outcome…" She paused a moment to nod her head gently up and down to drill in the point, "Consider my words very carefully, Horace; the choices you will soon have before you are not set in stone. You have the power within you to choose a different path. But that time is rapidly running out," she concluded, looking deep into his eyes.

"What?" said Horace, confused by what she had just said. Horace looked down at his drink, realizing that he felt a bit lightheaded from the laudanum that the elixir contained. He thought, *Maybe I can get lucky with this one? She seems to be nice enough to me… If I ask her up to my room, maybe she will accept?*

He looked back to her seat, with the words, *Do you want to 'ave a go of it?* still in his throat, was shocked to find that she was gone. He twisted his head around backward only to see her walking away down the hall. It struck Horace as odd that, with as many people milling about the hotel lobby as there were, not a single person noticed the nearly naked woman walking amongst them.

Once again rejected by a woman, was Horace's lone thought.

He got up from his stool with a sigh and walked to his room dejectedly. *I can't wait to be rid of this place... I can keep my own company,* he thought firmly as he made his way back alone.

The next morning, he stood outside the hotel, his steamer trunk in tow, waiting impatiently for Mr. Popovic and his wagon to take him back to the cemetery he called home.

III
HOW TO STUFF A PIG

It was a beautiful July day. The sun was shining, and all of nature had exploded in green growth with the coming of the heat and humidity of summer.

Horace, enjoying the day, was in the pig pen playing with Patty the Pig.

Horace loved Patty.

When he called, "Here Patty, Pig, Pig, Pig! Here Patty, Pig, Pig, Pig!" she would come running over to him, a big grin on her face. She would buck, hop, jump, and run in circles for joy at his call. He always had a treat for her, as he did now. "Here, Patty, Pig, Pig, Pig! I have peanuts for you!"

"Squeal! Squeal! Oink! Oink! Oink!" Patty said, anticipating the treat with glee. Horace took a handful of peanuts from his pocket and held them out for Patty. Patty gobbled them with delight, licking them up with her tongue from his flattened palm.

Horace enjoyed Patty's company so much that he decided Patty should live with him in the house. Despite his promise to himself to keep his own company after the disastrous experience at the Mortician's Convention, Horace found he was lonely and wanted a companion. He grabbed Patty by the ear and yanked her out of the pig pen, up the path leading to his house, and to the threshold of his kitchen. But at the doorway leading into his kitchen, Patty began to complain in earnest.

"Oink!" she yelled in protest. She bucked away from the door. Horace pulled her even harder by the ear to keep control of her.

"What in hell an' tarnation has got'n into ya Patty?" said Horace, struggling to control her. He pulled her back hard to the kitchen entrance.

"Oink! Oink! Oink! Squeeeeel!" Patty complained loudly, redoubling her efforts to escape. She bucked her hind legs hard.

"What's all this caterwauling you be makin'? You're gonna be a *guest* in my house; why all this noise?" Horace, redoubling his efforts, grabbed her right hind leg and yanked her hard, flipping her over onto her back. Quickly, before Patty could wiggle free, he snagged her hind legs at the ankles with one hand, and her front legs with the other, then lifted her to his chest, trapping her. With considerable effort to bear her heavy weight, Horace, grunting under the load, walked through the kitchen and passed through the door into the living room.

But as Horace was about to cross into the living room proper, Patty truly put up a fight. *"Squeeeeel! Squeeeeel! Squeeeeel!"* yelled Patty loudly as she bucked hard against her restraints with all her might.

"Now Patty, I just want you to sit with me on the couch so we can chat 'n such," said Horace as he strained to contain Patty. But Patty gave one last mighty buck and was free of his hold. Patty ran as if her legs were on fire, out of the house, and all the way back to the pig pen.

"Oink! Oink! Oink! Oink! Oink!" The sound of her cries receded in Horace's ears as she ran the distance.

Horace found her cringing at the very back of her little pig shed, hiding in the dark shadow of the far corner. He could see that she was shivering.

"What in the name of the Devil made you so cotton-pickin' afraid of in that there living room?" asked Horace to Patty as she continued to shiver in the dark.

Horace stepped back and sat on the stump of a tree as he looked in bewilderment at Patty's pig shed. He was next to the block he used to chop the heads off pigs during butchering time. The axe head was buried deep in the stump. As Horace looked at the stump, he recalled the loud squeal of the pigs he had slaughtered as they struggled against the inevitable; the sound of *Zing!* ringing out as the axe glided through the air in its arch towards the neck of the unfortunate pig, the *Whack!* as it hit, followed by the *Thump!* as their head hit the ground. The silence that followed always gave Horace a strange sense of peace. As he turned this memory of peacefulness over in his mind, Horace began to formulate an idea.

"Mayhap I could make Patty a bit calmer. Where she doesn't complain an' make such a racket when she is in the livin' room with me. Make 'er a good girl an' talk to me... forever like," pondered Horace with the seed of the idea floating about in his head. The seed suddenly sprouted into a full-blown idea that now gripped him. Horace quickly walked back to the house to develop the idea further.

Patty sat shivering alone in her shed. The man with the red eyes had been visiting her nightly for the past week. He told Patty that he had things to show her. Important things.

The man told me not to be scared of him, Patty recalled, *but he kept telling me that thing about '...the fate I am to endure but be not afraid because a reward shall come for me in the end...' or whatever it was. I didn't understand any of it. The scary man spoke kindly to me but his glowing red eyes scared the living crap out of me!* Patty shivered anew. *All those frightening images of Horace and his living room! Oink! What kind of reward could come from that?*

Patty had had nightmares all week about it. She cringed in the corner at the remembrance of those nightmarish visions.

I will never, EVER! go into that living room! No way, no how!

Six weeks had passed, and Horace was ready.

For the first two weeks, Horace pondered what he would need to bring his idea to life. He had learned bits and pieces of what he needed to know from the information he had gleaned from the various exhibits and lectures he had attended while at the Morticians Convention and Exposition, particularly the notes he had scribbled down from his conversation with the esteemed Egyptologist, Dr. Ingerson Schoefield.

In the following weeks, he made the ten-mile round trip to Columbia twice—first to order the necessary supplies, and then to pick them up.

Horace brought a large hand-pulled wagon for the return trip. He strapped the wagon handle around his waist using a leather strap so he could lug it like a sled dog. But the supplies were so heavy that the wheels dug into the dirt road, making the miles of pulling the wagon extremely labor-intensive. Horace had to stop mid-point to sleep the night, curling up in the grass of the road margin before he continued the next morning.

After arriving home, Horace arranged the items he had purchased on the kitchen tabletop. There were assorted bags, bottles, and tin cans. He sorted through 10 gallons of pine tar distillate, 10 gallons of 160 proof moonshine—Horace took a quick snort of the moonshine, swallowed then exclaimed in a hoarse voice, "Wowee! Great God in Heaven!" and after a cough and a moment to catch his breath he continued his work—5 gallons of eucalyptus oil, 5 gallons of garlic oil, 10 gallons of cedar oil, 5 pounds of powdered cinnamon, 4 pounds of myrrh resin, 2 gallons of canned beet juice, 50 pounds of salt, 50 pounds of granulated cane sugar, 10 pounds of powdered eucalyptus leaf, and 100 pounds of whole dried eucalyptus leaf.

Finally, he rolled the embalming table into the kitchen.

Satisfied he had everything in place that he needed, Horace grabbed his biggest and sharpest butcher knife and strode out the kitchen door towards the pig pen.

Patty, playing in the bright sunshine, did not see Horace approach from behind. Unfortunately for her, by the time she sensed him standing behind her, it was too late. She was blocked between him and the east corner of the pen. Panicking, she attempted to escape by running between his legs, but Horace had been prepared for this maneuver and squeezed his legs closed just at the pinch point of her waist, trapping her. Patty was a small pig, about 100 pounds, so it was no trouble for Horace—accustomed to lifting heavy loads—to grab her by the ear and hindquarters, flip her onto her back, and sit on her belly. She lay helpless as she watched Horace pull the long butcher knife from its scabbard.

"*Squeeeeel!*" she protested loudly as he drew the knife up to her neck, then cut her across from ear to ear, slicing her esophagus clean through, cutting open the left side carotid artery that ran the length of her neck. Blood gushed out of her carotid in great pulsating bursts.

"*Gurgle!*" Patty continued to protest as her lifeblood flooded her windpipe and spilled to the ground. As her blood drained, her protestation and thrashing soon quieted, then ceased altogether.

Patty was dead.

"Now she be a good girl," said Horace, looking down at her body. Much of her blood had splashed on him, but he paid this no mind.

Horace stood, grabbed a length of rope stowed to the side, and tied her hind feet together at the ankle. He then hoisted her up on his butchering tackle block. Her front legs and head dangled just above ground level. He drew his butcher knife once more and slit Patty's belly open down the middle from her crotch to her sternum. Her intestine unraveled and flopped to the ground with a wet splat.

Horace cut the various veins, arteries, intestines, and connective tissue separating her from her innards. Horace kicked the viscera out of his way so that he could wash her empty body cavity out with water he had brought with him in a bucket.

The other pigs, watching from the sidelines of the pen and knowing it was Patty's turn, ran over to the entrails and began greedily eating the offal. *"Oink! Oink! Oink!"* they cried excitedly as they ate. *Fresh Meat!* This was a rare treat for them.

After he finished washing Patty's carcass, Horace reached up and pressed the release mechanism for the tackle, sending her body crashing to the ground. He was about to pick her body up to carry her back to the house when he had a thought... He stepped over to the pile of innards, pushing the pigs impatiently to the side, reached into the bloody pile, and then cut her heart out from the mess. This he threw into Patty's chest cavity before picking her limp body up and carrying her out of the pen and up the dirt trail.

"Mayhap she be needin' her heart where she be going," Horace said aloud as he lugged her up the trail to the house.

Holding her up by her hind legs high enough so as not to drag her face on the ground, and panting from the effort, Horace duck-walked Patty's body all the way to the embalming table in the kitchen, where he dumped her. Patty the Pig lay on her back on the embalming table, splayed open for the world to view.

Horace began his work.

First, he sawed her head open with a backsaw and removed her brain. Then, with a giant glass syringe and needle the size of which only Dr. Frankenstein would appreciate, he flooded the subdermis of her skin, the meat of her muscle, and every vein and artery remaining in her body with a mixture of moonshine, pine tar distillate, cedar oil, and beet juice. Patty's skin inflated and turned pinkish. Horace then rubbed every exposed inch of her skin, inside and out, with a mush made of powdered eucalyptus and garlic oil. Next, he rubbed her skin with a mixture of powdered cinnamon, salt, and sugar. Patty looked like an Easter ham.

Finally, Horace filled Patty's body cavity with a mixture of finely ground eucalyptus leaves, wood chips soaked in pine tar distillate, cedar oil, salt, and sugar, finally sewing her body cavity shut with silk thread. He did the same with her skull cavity, sewing her skull cap back on when done.

When completed, Horace stepped back to admire his handiwork. Patty, even though her legs stood straight up and her eyes were glazed over, looked surprisingly plump, pink, and animated. Horace was pleased.

Placing Patty's feet up into a metal wash tub, he carried her out to the crematorium. He piled a mound of chopped eucalyptus leaves, soaked in cedar oil, onto the floor of the crematorium oven's chamber.

Onto a rig made of metal, Horace stood Patty upright, feet down, the rig holding Patty's right side up on top of the eucalyptus pile. He sprinkled myrrh resin over her and onto the pile of leaves around her, then closed the crematorium door. He turned on the gas and lit the pilot with a match. *Whoosh!* The flames went up from the burners. Horace turned the flames down to a very low setting before closing and locking the door tight.

Every four hours for the next three days, Horace returned to the crematorium to turn off the furnace burners, open the door, and add more myrrh resin, cedar oil, and powdered cinnamon to the pile. He brushed her skin with cedar oil and cinnamon, closed the door, and relit the burners. The smells that wafted out at each opening of the oven door very nearly overwhelmed Horace—dizzy, strong but not altogether unpleasant—reminding him of the perfume he had caught whiffs of in the rare times he had chanced a close encounter with a "fancy" city woman during his twice-yearly pilgrimages to Columbia.

On the evening of the third day, Horace turned off the burners for the last time. After waiting several hours for the oven to cool, he opened the steel door and stood a moment to examine Patty. When satisfied, he picked her up and carried her into the house. She was surprisingly light, having been fully desiccated. In a manner very similar to that of the ancient Egyptians, Horace had turned Patty into a mummy. However, unlike the withered mummies in the photos posted on Dr. Schoefield's lecture boards, because of the liberal application of oils to her flesh, Patty's skin remained amazingly soft and pliable. Her epidermis was soft leather and rather a beautiful dark tan in color. So supple was she that Horace could move her upper and lower leg joints and turn her head from side to side.

Like a large stuffed doll.

As a final step, Horace scraped out her dried, shriveled eyeballs from her eye sockets and replaced them with glass eyes he had procured from a novelty life-sized doll he had purchased in a toy store in Columbia. Had they known the purpose of his purchase, would they have sold him the doll? He thought that unlikely. Horace dressed Patty in a dress he had obtained from the same doll. He then sewed back the outer edges of her mouth, giving Patty a permanent smile. All things considered, Patty seemed to be in a rather happy mood. Horace picked Patty up, tucked her up under his arm (looking surprisingly like a large football), and carried her into the living room. He plopped her down onto the couch next to his favorite rocker and turned her head to look directly at him as he sat in his rocker.

Horace rocked quietly.

Horace looked at Patty… Patty looked at Horace.

"Well, Patty, how was your day today?" asked Horace to Patty.

"It was a rather trying three days, I am afraid to report my love," parroted Horace in a voice he imagined Patty would use if she could speak English.

"I'm so sorry, my friend, to have put you through all of that—it be necessary, you see, to help you with accepting being here with me in this living room. You understand, don't you?" replied Horace.

"Oh yes, of course I do. I know what you did for me was necessary. I can see the light. You could not have gotten me into this living room without you making this change to me. What a fuss I was making! Silly me," said Horace in the imagined voice of Patty.

This "conversation" continued in this vein for the rest of the evening. He chatted with her, and she "replied" to him in kind. Back and forth. Back and forth.

After several months of this "conversing," Horace had completely forgotten that Patty was a mummified pig. He had also forgotten that it was he who was answering for her. To Horace, Patty walked, pranced, conversed, and enjoyed their mundane exchange most animatedly and naturally. Horace was no longer alone. At last, he had found a friend.

IV
A GIRL TO CALL HIS OWN

During the dead of winter at the tail end of 1921, a powerful storm had swept across middle Tennessee. Freezing rain lashed down, the wind whipped the trees back and forth, lightning shattered the dark, and the resultant concussions of thunder shook the windows of Horace's humble home. Inside the living room, he and Patty, wrapped in blankets, waited out the worst of the weather. Patty was shaking with fear as the storm raged around them.

"Now, Patty, you've got nothin' ta worry yourself about. You'll be fine come the morning," said Horace, patting Patty on her head.

"I know that, but..." Patty began, but stopped abruptly at the sound of approaching hoofbeats, followed by a loud bray as a horse and wagon came to a halt just outside.

Horace peeked out the window and saw a man, his heavy coat and hat dripping wet with rain, slumped into his wagon seat, just sitting and staring at his hands. A forlorn look was upon his face.

Horace ran around to the entryway of the mortuary, threw on a pair of boots and a jacket, stepped out the door, and onto the mud of the parking area to greet the man.

As Horace approached the wagon, he could see the body in the box of the wagon covered by a blanket. From his sitting position on the seat cushion of the wagon, the man slowly brought his eyes up from his hands, turned to Horace, and said, "She be my daughter," before putting his head back into his hands to sob.

"Kind sir, I am Horace Graves, the owner of this here mortuary; I'm so sorry for your loss," said Horace to the man as gently as he could.

The man slowly, painfully, got up from his seat, clambered down to the ground, and walked to the back of the wagon. With a grim look on his face, he picked his daughter up in his strong arms across her rib cage and lower back, much like a forklift lifting a pallet. Her feet flopped down on one side, and her head and arms flopped down the other. Long, stringy blond hair almost touched the ground. She looked like a circus contortionist doing a backflip. Her jaw lay slack, broken off at one side, while her neck lay at a wrong angle at the mid-point of her throat, bruised, ruddy red and black.

Using hand gestures that communicated: *Follow me this way...* Horace led the man, carrying his dead daughter, from the wagon to the mortuary entrance. Horace made sure to lead him away from his personal entrance lest he see what was in the living room.

"My name is Eugene Schroeder, Kind Sir, an' this here," nodding downward with his head, "is my daughter Rose Schroeder. She be driving in 'er wagon when the horse spied a rattlesnake rattling at him an' he bucked up. So, my beautiful Rose was thrown clean off the wagon an' landed right on her head. This be the result of that fall.

Mr. Schroeder, looking down at Rose in his arms, returned to uncontrolled sobbing. Horace patted his back for a moment before gently lifting Rose from his arms to lay her down on the embalming table. Horace straightened her out as best as possible, then returned his attention to calming the distraught Mr. Schroeder.

"My poor, poor Rose! Oh! Thine Horrible and Unforgiving God Above! Please absolve my Rose of her sins and grant her a place in Heaven! She was a good girl. You know this be true!" cried out the grief-stricken Mr. Schroeder. Horace patted him on his back again. To Horace's surprise, the patting seemed to help a bit.

Horace saw that Rose was an unusually beautiful young woman and noted that she was about the same age as he was. He tucked these thoughts away for safekeeping as he had much work to focus on...

After Horace succeeded in calming the distraught Mr. Schroeder down, he and Mr. Schroeder made the necessary arrangements for the final showing and cremation of Rose. Horace showed Mr. Schroeder to the door.

"Now you remember to bring a dress you wish her to be viewed in by early tomorrow morn," said Horace as he closed the door behind him. He waited for Mr. Schroeder to walk back to the parking lot, unhitch the horse, mount the wagon, and yell "Giddy Up!" to spur his horse homeward.

Horace turned to look at Rose on the preparation slab.

Walking into his embalming room, Horace grabbed a pair of snips and used them to cut off her outer clothes; first, the dress, splattered with horse manure and blood, then her corset, followed by two layers of petticoat and slip. Finally, he cut off the underwear Rose wore around her nether region. Rose was naked and exposed to Horace.

Her head tilted at an unnatural angle. Horace worked his way around to the end of the table, grabbed her head, and pulled. Her neck made a series of loud popping sounds as her neck bones realigned. He then retrieved his needle and silk thread from the utility drawer nearby and stitched her jaw back in place onto her face.

Next, Horace cut a vertical incision, about one inch long,

down her neckline, below her ear, and toward the ridge of her shoulder. Using his index finger, he reached into the slit and pulled out a section of her carotid artery. This he cut in half. To the upper half, he inserted a cannula, the back side of which connected to a long rubber tube, which in turn connected to a pump. The pump came equipped with a tank, and the tank contained embalming fluid. To the lower half of the carotid artery, Horace inserted a second cannula connected to a rubber hose that dropped directly into a drainage bucket.

Horace cranked the pump handle. The red embalming fluid—the same formula his father had concocted—shot into her arteries and filled her body, both plumping her up and turning her skin from the gray-green of death to a glowing pink mimicry of life. When the embalming fluid started to flow into the waste bucket in earnest, he stopped cranking. He then pulled the cannula from the artery halves, pinching off the arteries with his fingers to keep the fluid from spilling out. He deftly clamped them shut with pinch clamps, then stuffed the artery halves back into her neck. Finally, he sewed the incision shut with silk thread.

For the next hour, Horace applied makeup to Rose's face and neck, making her look as if she were asleep, hiding the pallor of death, as well as the scars of injury.

The last thing Horace did that evening before retiring to the living room for the night was to sew Rose's orifices shut, *...so they don't make a mess in the viewin' chamber...* echoed his father's voice in his head.

He stood at the foot of the embalming table, gazing at Rose, her legs still spread from his labor down there.

It was late, and Patty had been calling him from the living room, "When are you going to come play with me, Horace? Aren't you done with her yet? Come *play*!" Horace looked longingly at Rose's body; his eyes going from her beautiful face, to her ample breast, and down to her exposed vagina. Face, breast, vagina, Face, breast, vagina. Face, breast, vagina.

"I want a wife!" Horace cried aloud.

Then in his thoughts:

Patty is a good companion an' I enjoy talkin' and playin' with her, but she be a pig! I have tried, but no woman will have me! This woman, Rose, has a kind face; I am sure she would have been nice to me. She be perty too! I bet she be a fine woman. Make someone a fine wife. Why not me? Why can't she be my wife?

With that, Horace, taking one last look at Rose, extinguished the wick lamps and retreated into the privacy of his living room to play with Patty…

…and to think of his future with Rose, though he said nothing of this to Patty. *No Sir!*

The next morning came. The Sun shone bright. The clouds had gone, and the sky was blue. The wind was still. A beautiful day had begun.

Eugene Schroeder knocked on the door below the sign reading *Office of the Graves Mortuary, Crematorium, and Memorial Park*. He was holding Rose's final clothing.

"This be her finest dress," said Mr. Schroeder, holding it out to Horace as Horace opened the door to answer.

"Rose will be ready for the viewing at ten this morning," replied Horace, lifting the dress from Mr. Schroeder's arms. "Please make yourself comfortable on the patio out back. There be refreshments out there," Horace pointed down the path where Mr. Schroeder was to go.

At ten o'clock, the viewing services began. Horace had Rose laid out in a simple pine box, the lid open. He had dressed her in a black new lace frock, a black cloche hat, white lace gloves, white lace ankle socks, and black Oxford tie shoes with gray accents, all provided by her father.

Her face was pink, beautiful (*I did a particularly good job with her makeup if'n I don't say so myself,* thought Horace as he looked down at Rose.) The mourners, eleven of the greater

Schroeder family, milled about the coffin. The consensus was that Rose looked lovely and at peace.

"My Rose loved the 'Flapper' style she did!" said Mr. Schroeder, "But I never am gonna git to take 'er to the big city to dance at one of their fancy clubs now," once again hiding his face in his hands, weeping loudly. And Horace once again found himself patting Mr. Schroeder gently on the back.

"Rose be a beautiful girl, Mr. Schroeder, and I know she be in heaven even now, dancin' with them gentlemen there!" comforted Horace. But his thoughts were with Rose dancin' with him.

After tea and cookies, the viewing concluded. When the Schroeder family had piled out of the viewing room, Horace closed the door behind them and watched through the curtain until every one of them had departed.

He returned to the viewing room and looked down at Rose.

A tight smile was on his lips.

HORACE WHEELED the casket back to the preparation room. Once there, he pulled Rose out of the casket and placed her on the slab. Horace walked to his workbench and selected his sharpest and longest butcher knife from the stack of tools. He dropped the knife into the bucket of his wagon, grabbed the wagon handle, and walked it to the door leading out to the back, the wagon wheels squeaking as it followed Horace out the door and to the grounds behind the house.

When he reached the pig pen, Horace opened the gate and stepped inside, pulling the gate closed behind him, the wagon in tow.

His pigs looked up at him expectantly. Most of the time, their master appeared either to feed them or to play with them. Sometimes, however, to their horror, he came to select one of them for slaughter. Unfortunately for them, this was one of those times.

Horace strode over to the sounder of swine and, quick as a cat, grabbed Jason, his biggest hog, by the hind legs. Before Jason could act, Horace brought the knife he had been hiding behind his back up to Jason's neck and slit the pig's throat from ear to ear. Jason, having expected some tasty treat, was more than a little surprised at seeing his own blood spill to the ground. Intending to complain at this grievous mistreatment with a loud *"Oooink!"* Instead, he could only manage a *"Kaaack!"* as he fell to the dirt, his head making a loud *whack!* as he hit the ground.

Horace, grunting from the effort of lifting the 120 pounds of dead pig, threw Jason into the bucket of the wagon. Horace rolled the wagon, made more difficult due to Jason's mass, redoubling his way back over the trail to his house, the wheels squeaking loudly in complaint the entire way.

Grunting loudly as he lifted Jason out of the wagon bucket, Horace dragged him across the floor and plopped him into the casket previously occupied by Rose. Horace slammed the casket lid shut and wheeled the gurney with the casket upon it out to the crematorium. Stopping to open the steel door, he then lined the gurney up with the crematorium opening and shoved the casket into the oven. Horace turned on the gas and lit the pilot. *Whoosh!* went the burners as the flames reached up and around the casket. Horace shut the door and locked it tight.

Horace was not entirely certain why he felt the need to carry out this charade of cremating a pig. After all, he reasoned, he could burn the casket or burn a bundle of wood kindling for that matter—a pile of ash is all that would remain. What would Rose's family know? *Perhaps,* Horace thought to himself, *if someone be looking, they would see me cart a heavy casket to the crematorium and think nothing is out of kilter. Perhaps it be okay to God if'n I sacrifice a pig in trade for the body of a young woman? Mayhap God celebrates if he receives a nice, fat pig to the glory of heaven instead of an innocent girl?*

He got to work without dwelling further on such things for the remainder of the evening.

Late the next day, after damping down the burners and allowing the kiln to cool, Horace returned to the crematorium, opened the door, lifted off the lid of a small brass urn he carried, and using a small paint brush, swept what little ash and bone remnants there were littering the oven floor into the urn. With the job completed, Horace closed the steel door, replaced the lid on the urn—later to be silver-soldered shut, ensuring its contents would never be exposed to prying eyes—and returned to the house.

He performed the funeral ceremony the following day. Horace had dug a small pit, roughly two feet square and three feet deep. After Horace said a prayer, Eugene Schroeder lowered the urn into the pit, and each member of the Schroeder family, one by one, lifted and poured a shovel of dirt into the hole. When the ceremony had concluded, the Schroeder family, crying in each other's arms, stepped into their wagons, mounted their horses, and made their trek homeward. Horace, waving the last goodbye from the entryway, closed the door behind him. He then walked to the preparation room where Rose lay.

HORACE LOOKED DOWN at Rose lying in repose on the embalming table, her final dress fitting perfectly and giving her a serene, dignified appearance. He carefully removed her clothing to prepare her for the next stage of the funeral arrangements, handling everything with respect and precision. "Let us begin," said Horace to Rose.

With that, he grabbed his butcher knife, cut her open from the top of her chest, where the neck met the plane of her clavicle, down between her breasts, clean through the thoracic diaphragm, down the middle of her abdominal cavity, stopping just at the Mons venues about one inch below the line of her pubic hair. With each hand, Horace grabbed the sides of the cut, and with a yank pulled Rose's body cavity clean open, exposing her viscera for the heavens to look upon.

UNSEEN BY HORACE, standing at the northeast corner of the memorial grounds, just below the giant oak tree that had stood in the graveyard for a hundred years, was Mr. Buchanan. Mr. Buchanan wore the very same suit, tie, hat, and shoes that he had been buried in one hundred very long years ago. The oak tree was but a young sapling when Mr. Buchanan's neighbor, Jim Maury, murdered him with an axe to the head. The blood and bits of brain, long dried, still stained the back of his suit and matted his hair around where the gash to his skull was located.

Mr. Buchanan had the distinct misfortune of being a member of the undead, and being undead meant being doomed to walk the graveyard grounds forever, or until the Devil decided to call him home, whichever came first. Most of the time, no one saw Mr. Buchanan wander the mortuary grounds, invisible to all but the occasional child, pig, or demon. But he could himself observe the world around him.

A thick metal chain looped around his neck. Attached to this loop of chain was a length of strong chain link four feet long, the other end of which a demon held—known to Horace and Patty the Pig as "The Man with the Red Eyes."

The name of this demon was Mr. Méchant.

Mr. Buchanan was riveted on the activities of Horace as he worked on Rose, spying the goings-on through the pane casement window mounted in the North wall of the mortuary work room. The light of an oil-wick lamp lit Horace's face as he quietly worked.

Mr. Méchant gave a hard yank to the chain to get the attention of Mr. Buchanan.

"Ye enraptured by what you see down there, Mr. Buchanan?" said Mr. Méchant in a deep sonorous voice. It was the hint of a growl that made his voice menacing.

"This be wrong, Mr. Méchant! What is a-goin' on down there be simple evil!" replied Mr. Buchanan.

Mr. Méchant, his eyes flashing brilliant red, laughed a belly laugh (in an equally menacing tone) and said, "Ah! Mr. Buchanan! Have you forgotten why ye are condemned to wander these here grounds with the walk of *de Mortvivant*? Need I remind you, Mr. Buchanan, of what you did to that young boy that drove the good Mr. Maury half mad with rage? Such rage that he smashed that axe into the back of your head?"

Mr. Buchanan, looking down at his feet, began to weep and plead.

"Please, Mr. Méchant, I beg of thee. Show me mercy... Put me out of this misery. I know not what I did with that boy. I be half out of my mind with that corn mash whiskey."

Mr. Buchanan fell to his knees, clasping his hands as if in prayer.

At this, Mr. Méchant slapped his knee as he belted out another bellow of laughter.

Mr. Buchanan shivered with fear as Mr. Méchant suddenly stopped laughing, stabbed his long forefinger at him, glaring down at him, the flames behind his eyes searing with heat, and said with a deep growl, "When the time comes, I will indeed free ye from this here Earth, Mr. Buchanan, my bete noire, and ye be then dancing in a lake of fire in MY abode. Your screams of agony I shall most enjoy."

Mr. Buchanan sobbed even louder.

Mr. Méchant yanked his chain hard once more, simply for

the pleasure of the pain he caused Mr. Buchanan. Mr. Méchant returned his gaze to Horace.

Had Horace looked up from his toiling and out the window to his right, he would have seen two red eyes, brightly lit against the dark black of the yard, staring directly back at him. But Horace was too absorbed in his work to look.

HORACE HAD EMPTIED Rose's body and skull cavities in the same manner as he had done to Patty. Her viscera and brain sat in the wash basin to the side of the embalming table. Her heart, now free from the gore, lay lonely in her body cavity. He rubbed her beautiful skin with the same oils, powders, and salts, flooded her flesh and veins with the same fluids, and filled her cavities with the same leaves and sugars he had used to preserve Patty. Finally, Horace sewed up her body cavity and stitched her skull cap back on with silk thread. Thus, completing the first part of Rose's mummification process.

Out at the crematorium, Horace suspended Rose from a wood pyre approximately one foot off the floor of the crematorium oven. On the floor, Horace had spread a thick layer of eucalyptus leaves saturated with oils. Finally, he liberally sprinkled myrrh resin about her body. He closed the door, locked it tight, and lit the burners. Horace set the flame low and returned home. Once there, he grabbed the basin containing Rose's guts and paid a visit to the pig pen.

Fresh Meat! The pigs grunted with joy as they ate with loud chomps.

Horace returned every four hours to check on Rose, to slather her in oils and spices, and to continue the smoking process.

By the end of the third day, Rose was as good as new.

Horace replaced her gray, shriveled remnants of eyes with glass eyes, and the process was complete.

Rose looked like the beautiful woman that she had been in real life. Almost.

Horace sat Rose on the couch next to his rocking chair and Patty to the left of her. Horace grabbed Rose's head with both hands and, with some effort, swiveled it around to look directly at where he sat. From his rocker, he could turn his head to look both Rose and Patty in the eye.

Horace announced, "Well, so I am to introduce the two of you, this bein' the first time you have met.

"Rose, this be my best friend Patty...

"Patty, this be Rose, my wife."

"Glad to make your acquaintance," said Rose to Patty demurely.

"Hello, Mrs. Graves," said Patty to Rose respectfully.

There was an awkward silence for a moment before conversation erupted between them in earnest.

The fantasy world Horace created had absorbed him so completely, that he had actively worried Rose and Patty would be too jealous of his affections to be in the same room with one another.

Horace sat back and relaxed. His "little family" was getting along quite well, thank you!

V
IS IT POLYGAMY IF BOTH ARE DEAD?

The weeks had passed. Horace was discussing the possibility of consummating the marriage with Rose, as Patty looked on.

"But Horace, my dear... You have sewn my female parts shut an' I am desiccated down there," said Rose delicately to Horace.

Horace, who had looked between Rose's legs to contemplate the possibilities with Rose, said, "Well, Great God Almighty! I never would have thought of this here eventuality."

"Well, my dear Horace. May I suggest an immoral act I learned while a teen student in France?

"It is involving my hand to replace the God-sanctioned carnal act of love..."

Horace, never having experienced *any* physical act of love with a woman, God-sanctioned or not, and having heard such acts from the bawdy talk of the men at the Morticians Convention, readily accepted.

As Patty turned her head away to allow them a modicum of privacy, the act ensued.

Horace could not believe how much pleasure there was in such things...

...HORACE REPEATED this act nightly for several months before the novelty wore off.

THE STORM FRONT crossed middle Tennessee. The sign *Office of the Graves Mortuary, Crematorium, and Memorial Park,* whipping back and forth in the winds of the storm, slapped the side of the mortuary home with a loud *bang! bang! bang!*

Lightning snaked its way from cloud to ground and crawled along the cloud bottoms as the storm blew its way eastward. Thunder shook the house as Horace, Rose, and Patty waited out the worst of the storm's fury in the living room. It was then that Horace heard weeping coming from the entry to his property. Horace lifted the window blind and looked out toward the front.

When the next lightning flash illuminated the acre of land leading from the house's entryway, Horace saw a man pulling a wagon. The man was sobbing so hard that he stumbled and fell forward to lie prone in the mud. Horace ran out the door and to the front to help.

As Horace reached the wagon, he could see that in the back of the wagon were two bodies, one a female adult and the other a tiny newborn baby. When Horace approached, the man pulled himself up from the mud, rose to his knees, and then stood fully, dripping with mud from his feet to his hat. "I be Frank Wilkinson, an' this be my wife Evelyn an' baby Anna still in 'er arms," the man said as Horace approached, pointing to the two bodies.

"What happened to 'em?" asked Horace gently.

Mr. Wilkinson replied, "They die in the efforts of birthin'. We were waitin' for the midwife to show up, but the storm come an' slow her progress. Evelyn went into birth before the midwife could make 'er way an' Anna be a breech birth…

"… The cord be around 'er neck…"

Mr. Wilkinson began to sob as he spoke, forcing Horace to concentrate hard to understand him, "… an' strangle 'er as she coming 'er way down 'er momma's birthin' canal.

"Unfortunately for poor Evelyn, 'er insides be all badly torn up an' she bleed bad.

"The midwife showed up just in time to see 'em dead…

"… Sad day.

"I come here fast as I can to see my Evelyn an' my baby Anna be buried proper like," finished Frank.

"You come to the right place, you did, Mr. Wilkinson. I'll be taking good care of your Evelyn an' Anna here. They be in good hands."

Horace walked over to the wagon, slung Evelyn over his shoulder with his left arm, and grabbed Anna in his right arm, clamping her tight to his chest. He duck-walked back to the mortuary, the legs of Anna swinging with each step he took.

"I'll see you in the mornin' for the final arrangements, Mr. Wilkinson. Now you git homeward and try to fetch ya some sleep!" Horace shouted over his shoulder towards Mr. Wilkinson as he trudged.

Mr. Wilkinson held a grim face as he circled to the front of the wagon, grabbed the handle, and trundled homeward with shoulders slung low and feet dragging with the weight of his grief.

AFTER DROPPING the limp Evelyn onto the embalming table and placing Anna on a spare spot on the counter, Horace returned to the living room to discuss an idea with Rose that he had been mulling over for the last several weeks.

"My dearest Rose," Horace began, a bit nervous about introducing the topic he was about to propose, "you know I love you with all me heart—but the immoral act we've been performin' just ain't a normal act of physical love between a husband an' wife... If'n I'd been more aware of how the world works an' things, I wouldn't 'ave sewed your nether region shut as I done. But now this be too late to change things, being what they are...

"So, because of this, I was thinkin' bout bringin' in another wife into our little family we have us here."

"Are you sure this be necessary, my dearest husband? Patty an' I be about as happy as bugs in a rug just the three of us here together," Rose replied with a timid tone to her voice.

"I know you be speaking the truth, my Love, but there be a space on this couch, and an empty place in my heart," finished Horace.

After some further discussion, they reached a decision. Patty and Rose were eager for Horace to carry out his plan.

MR. WILKINSON RETURNED the following afternoon to meet with Horace and talk over the burial plans.

"I not want any fussin' Mr. Graves. I can't bear to see my sweet Evelyn and innocent Anna laid out with the look of death upon them. No matter how you make them up, they be dead.

"No viewing, no open caskets for me," said Mr. Wilkinson, a look of finality on his face.

"An' it only be me at the services—no relatives exceptin' me drunk of a brother in Pennsylvania—the rest of me family still be livin' in the Old Country.

"It be closed caskets and a quick service for Evelyn and Anna; they are in Heaven by now, I's supposin', so no matter anyways," finished Mr. Wilkinson, a tear running down his face.

"There be no problem with that, Mr. Wilkinson, no problem at all. I will see to everything. Come back day after morrow an' it be done," said Horace with as gentle a tone as he could muster.

Horace got to work on Evelyn the moment Mr. Wilkinson had mounted his gelding and ridden home.

By the time Mr. Wilkinson returned, Evelyn was desiccating in the crematorium, well on her way to mummification, this time with her nether region not only left intact but especially well-oiled.

When he completed the process the following morning, Horace planned to place Evelyn at the spot on the couch nearest him, and to move Rose and Patty over, and further from him. Horace assumed that this spot was always meant for Evelyn—he hoped Rose would not be too jealous of the seeming demotion in the pecking order to this arrangement.

Horace had sacrificed another pig to take Evelyn's place—"one for one," he had consoled himself—and now that pig lay in the casket. The brass nameplate nailed to the front of the casket declared *Rest in Peace, Evelyn Wilkinson.* A baby-sized casket of identical design lay beside a smaller pit dug to the right of Evelyn's presumed coffin, but in this case, the casket actually did contain the remains of Baby Wilkinson.

Mr. Wilkinson had noticed the smoke coming from the crematorium and smelled the very pungent fragrance emanating from its smokestack. He did not think much of the fact that Horace had the crematorium working—*he must be a busy Mortician to have a whole other set of customers to contend with,* he thought to himself, *but that smell be very odd…* Never having been near a crematorium in operation, however, he was not quite sure if that was simply the way things smelled.

Mayhap morticians add special herbs to help with the burnin'? He thought, attempting to rationalize this, but felt instead an odd sense of foreboding. He shook himself out of his ruminations and returned his attention to the service.

With the conclusion of a simple prayer by Horace, and with Mr. Wilkinson quietly bowing his head as he wept quietly over the coffins, Horace began the task of turning the crank that would lower Evelyn's casket into the ground.

Unexpectedly, Mr. Wilkinson blurted out: "Wait! Stop! I want to see my Evelyn and say goodbye one last time. Open the coffin!"

"But. But. But..." Horace spluttered, "I can't. I mean, you can't. I mean, it's not possible!"

"What are you blathering on about? Open the God-forsaken coffin!" spat out Mr. Wilkinson.

"The coffin is nailed shut. It's sealed. Rose... I mean, Evelyn has begun to rot somethin' awful, Mr. Wilkinson. She'd be purple an' green by now!" exclaimed Horace in a panic.

Thankfully for Horace, that imagery was enough to squelch the protestations of Mr. Wilkinson long enough for Horace to lower Evelyn into the burial pit.

The gears whined and squealed as Horace turned the crank at a frantic pace, lowering the casket into the ground as fast as he could muster. With the casket fully lowered, Mr. Wilkinson witnessed Horace throw shovel full after shovel full of dirt into the grave, seemingly, to Mr. Wilkinson's sensibilities, at a pace resembling nothing short of hysteria.

As Mr. Wilkinson watched Horace rush to bury his wife, the strong sense of foreboding returned.

He behavin' so strange a manner... Somethin' be very wrong here, thought Mr. Wilkinson, but he was unable to put his finger on what, exactly, was wrong.

For Mr. Wilkinson, however, the sense of foreboding continued in him long after he returned home and lingered long into that evening.

Phew! That's about as close a call as you can get, thought Horace after seeing Mr. Wilkinson off, believing he'd just dodged a bullet.

That evening, after Horace had washed up, said goodnight to Rose and Patty, and said his evening prayers, he lay his head on his pillow and closed his eyes. He wanted the morning to come as quickly as it could. Evelyn was waiting.

In the morning, Horace rushed out to the crematorium to shut down the burners. He impatiently waited for the oven to cool so he could open it and retrieve his bride. Soon, he had her in the embalming room to complete the final preparations and afterward, to dress her. He was tingling with excitement as he hurried into the living room to place Evelyn at her designated spot. He made the appropriate introductions all around. Then it was time.

Time, thought Horace, *to finally lose my virginity—Evelyn is ready and waiting...*

And, as Rose and Patty looked on, this time without modesty, Horace pulled Evelyn's dress up over her head, pulled her panties off, and spread her legs. He then slicked up his member and her vagina with lard, her vagina already made pliable by his extra oil treatments during her mummification and eagerly consummated the marriage with his new wife.

The couch thumped with his enthusiastic thrusts.

Horace collapsed, sweaty and happily exhausted after the

act, into his rocker. *A second wife. How fortunate I am,* thought Horace as he sat and gently rocked.

Evelyn, Rose, and Patty smiled and giggled quietly—covering their mouths with their hands in pleasant humor whenever Horace looked their way.

IN THE MIDDLE of that same night, Frank Wilkinson lay in his bed having a nightmare. In it, he was awake and standing next to his bed, still in his bedclothes. Just then, a man—no… not a man…but some kind of monster, with eyes that burned like fire, walked into his bedroom and approached him. He shivered in fear but was unable to move as this man, *this demon!* slowly approached, stopping short a foot directly in front of Frank. Frank noted how tall this man was and how long his face and fingers were.

"Good evening, Mr. Wilkinson. Allow me to introduce myself. I am Mr. Méchant," began the demon.

Mr. Méchant brought his long index finger up, the long fingernail pointed and dark, and with his finger, he made a 'follow me' gesture to Frank, "I've got something to show you, Mr. Wilkinson. We'll be taking a walk now," Mr. Méchant said in his gravely sonorous voice.

I am havin' a most vivid dream, I am, thought Frank, with no small amount of dread as he began to follow Mr. Méchant.

I am followin' without much protest it appears, as my body seems to have a life of its own; as if this Mr. Méchant have some kind of power over me, as Frank walked in his night clothes, *must be because this only be a dream; If'n this was real, I be screamin' and runnin' for my life!*

As he reached the door leading from his bedroom to the kitchen, he looked back and saw himself still asleep in bed. *Most peculiar dream this be,* considered Frank.

As he continued to follow, he felt the cold air as he

stepped out of his front door and into the yard. He looked up and saw the night sky was brilliant with stars, and the full moon shone bright, lighting up the landscape with soft light.

"This seems so real! I feel as if I am speaking out loud to you!" he commented with consternation as he followed tentatively behind Mr. Méchant.

"So, this seems. So, this seems, my good Mr. Wilkinson. Now don't you be lollygagging! We don't have much time before the sun comes up to show you what it is that I have to show you," replied Mr. Méchant over his shoulder to Frank.

Frank was surprised when he stepped off his yard to what he thought would be the dirt road leading to Springdale. He found himself instead stepping on the dirt path at the North end of Horace Graves's property.

I must have been drifting off to sleep the five miles between my house an' here... Mayhap I be flying—would a liked to have remembered that! Frank thought to himself in surprise.

It was then that he realized Mr. Méchant was leading him to his wife's grave.

"She was buried only just day before yesterday," said Frank, stating the obvious. Mr. Méchant paid no mind to this as he led Frank up the path to her grave.

Seeing a little girl—he guessed about four years old—sitting on top of a granite tombstone near his wife's fresh grave, her feet pulled close as she balanced on the flat of the tombstone shocked Frank. *What in the name of Hell is a little girl doin' here at this time of night?* thought Frank in surprise. Frank read the writing chiseled into the tombstone below where the little girl sat:

Our Darling Little Princess
Francesca Anne Harpeth
born 1852 died 1856
Her Soul Rests Now and Forever
In Heaven

. . .

THE LITTLE GIRL was wearing a formal dress and patent leather shoes, but was otherwise ignoring the chill of the night air. The girl waved a quick "Hello" with her left hand to Frank as she sat quietly watching them. Mr. Méchant tipped his hat to her with a formal "Miss Harpeth" aloud before continuing to lead Frank to the head of his wife's grave. The girl nodded a barely noticeable acknowledgment back to Mr. Méchant.

"You will not let that Mr. Horace Graves know that I have brought you here, or ye will face my wrath," warned Mr. Méchant, A deep growl rumbled from his voice, and the red of Mr. Méchant's eyes bore into him, sending a shiver down Frank's spine. "Now get ye down onto your knees, Mr. Wilkinson!" Mr. Méchant demanded loudly, stabbing his long forefinger toward the grave.

Frank looked at Mr. Méchant with a shocked look on his face, only managing to get out a, "You want me to do what?" in reply.

"Get yourself down on your knees, Mr. Wilkinson, I want you to hear something down there," Mr. Méchant repeated ominously.

Frank decidedly did not like this Mr. Méchant—in fact, he scared the living hell out of Frank—but he reluctantly complied nonetheless, slowly lowering himself to the ground, first squatting on his haunches, then dropping to his knees the final inch or so to the ground. He heard nothing and looked up at Mr. Méchant with a questioning look on his face.

"Now put your ear down on your wife's grave..." Mr. Méchant said, signaling with his long forefinger, "... Down you go."

So, Frank placed his left ear on the ground directly above where (he thought) his dead wife's head lay six feet down. It was then that he heard the faint voice...

"I'm *so cold... so cold...*" A soft sobbing followed, then "Help me! I'm trapped and helpless... Get me out of this dark and evil place. Please help me!" came the soft pleading voice.

Frank sat up, clapped his hands together in prayer, tilted his face to the sky, and in a beseeching voice yelled, "Oh my Great an' Horrible God, please help my poor Evelyn; she is trapped in 'er grave! Please, I beg of thee! Help me rescue her!"

Sobbing uncontrollably, he began to claw at the dirt of the grave, pulling up handfuls and throwing the moldering ground to the side.

FRANK WOKE near dawn with a start and screamed out loud, "Evelyn!" He was grasping at his blanket, pulling at it as if he were pulling out invisible clumps of dirt.

Frank looked around; he was alone in his bedroom in the same position in his bed as he was when he went to sleep. He wore the same bedclothes that he had put on the prior evening before retiring to bed. He looked down at his hands; they were clean. His bed sheets were unsoiled.

He knew what he needed to do.

The dream was so vivid that Frank felt it must be some sort of message; he *knew* his Evelyn had been buried alive. Frank got up immediately from his bed, dressed, marched out to his barn to grab a shovel, and to throw a saddle over his horse. He galloped the five miles to The Graves Mortuary, Crematorium, and Memorial Park, stopping just short of the property, his intuition telling him not to alert Horace as to his intentions. Frank tied his horse to a tree about a quarter mile upwind from Horace's house. He walked quietly the rest of the way to the mortuary property carrying the shovel.

Frank was tiptoeing past the house by the living room window when he heard Horace talking animatedly. He noted that there were neither horses on the hitch, nor was there a wagon in the yard.

Who in the name of the Great Jehovah Above is Horace talking to? Well... No matter, he was in his house an' not out in the graveyard grounds, thought Frank as he quietly slid past the window.

He made his way quickly to the north end of the graveyard.

Reaching her grave, he quickly got to work. At a rapid pace, he kicked the shovel scoop into the soft dirt of his wife's grave, lifting the shovel and dumping the dirt to the side. He continued digging for the next two hours with only a quick pause every so often to crack his sore back. *My back be a burning wreck of pain tomorrow, as God be my witness,* thought Frank.

By the time the Sun was firmly above the tree line and blasting Frank's head with heat, he was sweaty from his effort. The sweat ran in rivulets down his face and dripped off the ridge of his jawline, soaking his shirt front.

He had almost dug his way to her coffin.

Despite the blisters that were rising on his palms, he continued to dig fervently for another fifteen minutes, then: *thump!,* his shovel hit wood.

Frank spent the next half an hour absorbed in the task of sweeping the last vestiges of dirt from the lid of her coffin. To lift the coffin lid, however, Frank had to climb out of the hole, lie flat upon the earth above it, and reach with his right arm all the way down into the hole, grabbing his wife's headstone for support. When he had reached the entire depth of the pit, and his hand could take hold of the coffin lid, with a great sweating effort, he pulled the lid up as hard as he could.

"*Geeeuuuunnn!*" he grunted as his teeth gnashed at the strain to open the lid.

The lid gave way and creaked as it opened.

"Nailed shut my ass," Frank exclaimed as he lifted the lid fully upright.

Frank looked inside the coffin.

"What the Shit!"

Frank rarely cursed, but as he looked down at the dead pig that occupied the coffin his wife was supposed to be in, he simply could not control his outburst. Frank got up on his haunches, intending to march into Horace's house and demand an explanation.

The head of the five-pound sledgehammer, welded by an unseen assailant from behind him, hit Frank's head at precisely that moment, cracking Frank's skull clean open, and sending bits of Frank's skull, bone, and gray matter into the grass. The bits and pieces made a sickening little *splat!* sound as they splattered on the ground.

Frank hit the ground hard face first nearly falling into his wife's open grave. He dropped into a deep, dark coma. Moments later, his heart began to palpitate, and then shortly after that, it stopped beating altogether. Frank lay dead.

HORACE LOOKED DOWN at the gore that remained of Frank's head and said, "God have mercy on his soul," in a solemn, but not entirely sincere tone.

Horace flipped Frank's face up, grabbed him by the lapel of his shirt, then lifted him, slinging him over his shoulder.

"I'll have to come back to bury the coffin again before someone sees the mess you've made, Mr. Wilkinson," Horace grunted to Frank's dead body as Horace walked with effort up the trail; Frank was almost too large and heavy for Horace to manage.

But, thankfully for Horace, years of graveyard labor made him able to lug dead weight. Frank's feet, dragging on the ground, Frank being tall and Horace short, left little indentation marks like a trail marker that read "This way to Hell," as Horace trudged his way to the house.

It was not long after that, that the profanation of Evelyn's grave was once again buried deep in dirt, covered up for the hereafter. And Frank, now mummified, sat at the last open spot of Horace's couch, the newest member of Horace's dark little menagerie.

"I am so glad you could join us for our private little tea party this afternoon, Frank," said Horace.

"Oh yes, I agree!" said Rose in excitement.

Patty nodded in agreement, and Evelyn clapped with excitement, a large smile on her face.

"Why of course. I am delighted to join you on this fine day," said Frank with excitement.

What a wonderful thing this is! My life couldn't be more perfect! Horace thought with excitement as he looked around at his friends, *his true friends,* he corrected himself, friends who shared his living room. Horace glowed at being the center of their affection. They sipped their tea and chatted the afternoon away.

VI
THE STRENGTH CARD

Francesca Anne Harpeth, forever four years old, was sitting on top of her tombstone, her feet dangling over the edge. She was kicking the granite face. Next to her grave was the grave of her mother, Anne Grace Harpeth, buried twenty years after her death.

Francesca had died of cholera, while Dropsy had taken her mother.

Francesca's family members still visited Francesca and Anne's graves from time to time. The day before, on a beautiful sunny Sunday, relatives of Francesca's (Francesca did not know who they were), William Harpeth, and his wife, Julia Harpeth, had come to visit his Great Auntie's grave, their three-and-a-half-year-old son in tow.

"Look, Ralphie," said Julia, attempting to get the attention of her son, "there is the grave of your Great Aunt, Anne Grace Harpeth, and her daughter Francesca Harpeth right next to her. They were buried here a long, long time ago..."

Julia had opened an antique picture book that contained a photo of Francesca framed on the left side and Great Anne Grace framed on the right. "Lookie here, Ralphie! See their pictures? Weren't they beautiful?" but her enthusiastic tone failed to catch the attention of young Ralph

Ralph's attention was instead on that of the ghost of Francesca.

Francesca, standing near the small group, waved a small hello to Ralph. He thought she looked sad. He said a cheerful "Hi!" to Francesca in return, with the hopes of making her smile. She did.

Julia, wondering who Ralph was saying hello to, said, "Who are you talking to, sweetie?"

"The girl mama... The girl in the picture. She's standing right over there!" Ralph was emphatically pointing to the picture of Francesca and then pointing to Francesca herself.

The mother looked every which way for a girl in the graveyard but could see no one else around. A shiver went down her spine.

"Let's go, Bill. I want to get out of this place," she said to her surprised husband. She snatched up little Ralphie and walked rapidly towards the graveyard exit.

"But Mommy, I want to play with the little girl. Let me go!" said Ralphie in a tone that both Julia and Bill knew as the preamble to him pitching a fit.

"Time to go Ralphie. How about we go to the playground... Your favorite playground by our house. All your friends will be there," Julia intoned with enthusiasm hoping this would forestall a screaming jag. But on the way out, her hair stood on end, and she intuitively knew something was wrong. She wanted out of the graveyard and pronto.

Francesca waved bye to Ralph as she watched Julia rush him away.

Her confused husband followed reluctantly behind, a puzzled look on his face. *Did she see a snake?* he wondered to himself, though he saw none as he scanned the grass about the graves. *But the day is so nice and this place so quiet,* he added to himself as he continued to follow his wife and son out of the graveyard grounds.

FRANCESCA, as she had every morning since her mother's burial sixty-six years prior, attempted to wake her mother.

"Mother. MOTHER! Are you down there? Wake up, Mother! I want to play!" Francesca yelled at the ground directly atop her mother's grave in the hopes her spectral voice would make it all the way down to the casket buried six feet below.

But to no avail.

Unlike Francesca, Anne had departed the world for good when *she* died.

But, as was the case with Mr. Buchanan, Francesca was a member of the undead. The similarities ended there, however. Although Francesca could see Mr. Buchanan (she instinctively knew how to keep a wide berth from him), Mr. Buchanan could not see her. Additionally, and most importantly, Mr. Méchant had no vested interest in her. In fact, Mr. Méchant showed much kindness to her, mostly by greeting her with "... Hello, my pretty little Francesca, I hope this day is treating you well?" tipping his hat as he walked past her on his way to do some very nasty, unpleasant business.

But sometimes he would bring a game of checkers for them to play. Mr. Méchant would balance the checkerboard on the top of Francesca's tombstone, he standing to one side, and Francesca at the other, as they took turns at the game. Mr. Méchant would always let Francesca win. Francesca, in great joy at yet winning again, would jump up and down, her beautiful patent leather shoes click-clicking as she jumped, clapping her hands in excitement, "Yeah! Yeah! Yeah! I won! I won! I won!"

Mr. Méchant would beam a broad smile then reply to her, "You did my petite Mort Vivant. You did."

Francesca did not know what "Mort Vivant" meant, but

she knew that "petite" meant small, so she guessed the term was "My little love" as her father had often liked to call her.

Francesca liked it when Mr. Méchant came to visit her, but she did not like what was happening *in THAT room!* She knew Mr. Méchant had a connection to *THOSE THINGS* and wanted him to promise her that Mr. Graves would leave her alone.

Sometimes, despite her great fear and deep revulsion of them, she would wander down the path that led to Mr. Graves' house, then creep into the living room where the mummies lay. She could see their ghosts entombed in their desiccated bodies, but to Francesca's puzzlement, they appeared unable to escape them.

On one of these visits, one of the mummies (Rose) had said to her in a spectral voice: "Hi there, pretty little girl. Are you coming to visit us again? Please stay and play."

That scared little Francesca so much that she turned and ran as fast as her ghost legs could take her back to her grave. When she reached her burial site, she dove into the ground, flying through the dirt the six feet it took to reach her coffin to hide, ignoring her own moldering corpse that shared the confined space with her. She never returned to the living room again.

"You promise me that Mr. Graves won't do *THAT* to me?" she asked Mr. Méchant with obvious fear in her eyes.

"You needn't worry your pretty little head about that, my dear Francesca. You will not be bothered by the likes of Mr. Graves. I promise," Mr. Méchant replied, holding his hand to his heart.

She had witnessed Mr. Graves bash the back of Mr. Wilkinson's head in with a sledgehammer and then carting the poor Mr. Wilkinson away to *THAT ROOM!* All the while, the discorporate soul of Mr. Wilkinson, to avoid that awful fate, ran after his physical self, in a desperate attempt to grab his body and yank it back, only to find his fingers no longer able to grasp the objects of the physical world. His pleading: "Nooooooo! God please! Nooooooo!" from Mr. Wilkinson as he ran after, had pulled at Francesca's heartstrings.

She cried for the three days that followed while Mr. Graves was at work. Now, the *AWFUL THING* was done, and there was nothing else to do… Francesca sat on top of her tombstone, kicking the back of her left shoe into the granite of the tombstone. *Click! Click! Click!* went her shoe heel.

THE SUMMER AIR that morning was cool but clear. The sky was cloudless; the Sun was just peaking over the edge of the world, bathing the headstones in the graveyard with a golden glow. A gentle wind blew the tree branches, and the rustle it made through the tree leaves sounded like the dull ring of a million wind chimes. Every living thing was waking up to say good morning to the Sun.

Over by the tree line near where Francesca sat on her tombstone, birds began to gather. A few goldfinch and robins at first, but then soon after by the hundreds: blue jays, chickadees, wrens, juncos, woodpeckers, and crows lined every branch of every tree for a thousand feet around her.

Earthworms, red wigglers, millipedes, pill bugs, slugs, and snails by the thousand dug up from the earth or crawled out from under rocks and downed rotted tree limbs, wiggling and crawling—struggled as they did on the cool of the ground, drawn from the safety of their muddy nests and cubbyholes because... She was coming.

Bumble bees, wasps, butterflies of every color and stripe, fireflies, green darners, and dragonflies flitted and flew in lazy loops around the graves, making *buzz!* noises with the frantic flutter of their wings.

Acorn weevils, garden spiders, stinkbugs, fire ants, and locusts by the millions crawled up the tree trunks in swarms and clumps.

Salamanders, alligator lizards, copperheads, garters, and red corn snakes crawled, darted, and slithered onto the grass nearby.

A multitude of foxes, raccoons, skunks, bobcats, and white-tailed deer soon joined the party. Tiny brown mice bobbed and jumped.

What was calling them? The creatures knew and could feel the energy building. They could not describe to you or me what exactly it was that was coming; they just knew down to their very DNA. A powerful call it was, and they wanted to be as near to the center of *Her* as possible.

Francesca sat passively watching the gathering of creatures around her feet. The ground and canopy surrounding where she sat were alive with motion.

She did not need the animals to tell her what was happening; however, she had seen this before and knew what was next... Ariel was coming for a visit.

Between two closely spaced tree trunks, a million insects gathered.

Ants, locusts, beetles, and millipedes grabbed the claw, mandible, wing, and leg of the adjoining insect to form a web. Spiders knitted from insect to insect with a silk thread to hold the growing form fast. They climbed and joined, forming a curtain of intertwined tiny insectile bodies until a living curtain stood six feet tall.

Suddenly, beautiful human female hands stabbed out through the curtain and parted it neatly down the middle. When the curtain separated into two, Ariel stepped out into the graveyard grounds.

Ariel stood up with her back straight and tall like a graceful ballet dancer. She appeared every bit the vision of gentle strength. She wore a wrap of colorful fine mesh silk scarves: white, red, green, yellow, and blue. Her naked body was visible through the sheer cloth.

She had a simple, unadorned, yet mature beauty to her face. Her feet were bare. On her head, a wreath of flowers adorned the soft waves of her long, brunette hair. She was not fat, but bore the fullness of a woman most men would think favorably upon seeing her: *Now that is a woman for bearing children...* Ariel smiled at Francesca as she folded her intelligent, smooth hands to her lap before her.

"Hello once again, my child," she said to Francesca.

"Yeah! You came!" Francesca yelled in excitement as she jumped to the ground and ran to Ariel. When she reached her, she wrapped her arms around Ariel's legs in a loving embrace.

The creatures crawling the ground around her feet had no fear she would crush them, and made attempts to escape her footfalls, for they felt nothing of Francesca's spectral presence.

ARIEL SPENT the rest of the daylight with Francesca. They talked of the new year to come. They talked of Mr. Méchant and their pleasant games of checkers.

"He even lets me win," clapped Francesca with delight. Ariel smiled in return.

They talked of Francesca's mother.

"Where is she, Ariel? I call an' call an' call an' still she sleeps. When will she wake up?" said Francesca with a tear forming in her eye.

"I have told you this before, my young child, your mother is beyond the curtain..." Ariel pointed back to the curtain of insects that Ariel had stepped through.

"... And that is where you should be, my beautiful Francesca," finished Ariel.

"I know this, Mrs. Ariel. But Mr. Méchant tells me that life here on this Earth is an amazing thing to witness… Especially as I am… A spirit, because I feel no pain! And I get to play *forever*—I will never have to grow up—Ever."

"Yes, my child—Mr. Méchant speaks truth…

"But don't you want to see your mother again, my darling?" asked Ariel kindly.

At that, Francesca looked down at her feet and said nothing.

"Ariel?" began Francesca timidly.

When Ariel looked at her expectantly, Francesca replied:

"Are you going to stop that wrong that is down there in that living room?" came the question, Francesca pointing in the direction of Horace's house, the sheer terror of the current events written clear as murder on Francesca's face.

"I cannot, my darling. But when the time comes, I will be here to help them," said Ariel, turning her head to look down the path towards the house.

"You promise, Ariel? Pinkie swears?" said Francesca, and she held out the pinkie finger of her left hand to Ariel.

"I promise you I will do this," said Ariel, crossing her own pinkie with that of Francesca's.

Francesca thought for a minute about the atrocity just a stone's throw from her grave and clasped her two hands together, saying in a barely audible voice, "… Mrs. Ariel, I am not ready just yet for the other side; I still wish to stay here a bit longer… I want to know if that Mr. Graves gets what is comin' to 'im," Francesca crossed her arms in front of her chest in defiance.

Ariel kissed Francesca on her forehead and gently placed Francesca's hand in hers. "So be it. I bid you goodbye for now, my sweet little girl."

Ariel got up, waved a silent goodbye, and then walked to the insect curtain, parting it with both hands. She walked through and disappeared into the beyond.

The slice in the insect mesh closed, and the insects quickly reformed a barrier. Just as suddenly, the curtain of insects fell into a pile. The insects, invertebrates, birds, and mammals, just as quickly as they had gathered, scattered to their normal lives.

VIII
ET TU, BRUTE?

Fall was typically busy for Horace, and this fall was no exception. The farmers in and around *The Graves Mortuary, Crematorium, and Memorial Park* were busy harvesting their crops, and Death was busy harvesting people. Horace had his work cut out for him.

Gloria O'Neil, who died of consumption, was lowered into the ground in a grand, solid oak casket shipped all the way from New York City. Her gaggle of twelve children, four uncles, five aunts, and dozens of nieces, nephews, cousins, and second cousins crowded around the casket, talking loudly as they remembered family events and the eccentricities of Gloria. They shared memories affectionately, as all present considered Gloria to be an adorable person, with a pinch of lunatic.

Father Whittaker, from the Second Coming of Christ Ministries in Franklin, presiding at the funeral of Mrs. O'Neil, was reading from the bible in a somber tone. After the conclusion of the burial ceremony, Horace guided them up to the patio area behind his house for tea and cookies. In all, *a rather pleasant group of people,* Horace thought, after which he saw them off homeward with a friendly, "Goodbye and safe travels!"

After lunch, while throwing the final few shovelfuls of dirt out of the grave he dug for Patrick Jebson—Patrick had died quietly in his sleep due to a massive heart attack, commonly referred to as a "widow maker"—the steel blade of his shovel hit the dirt wall separating Patrick's grave is with that of Ol' Mrs. White. The ground gave way due to how tightly packed the graves were in this section of the cemetery. Ol' Mrs. White, who had been in the ground for more than one hundred years, and with her coffin clean rotted through, the skeletal remains of her body, still in the moldered dress her loved ones buried her in, tumbled out and onto Horace's foot. Horace, not missing a beat, picked her remains up and threw them back into her casket and continued with his work.

That afternoon, a group of the True Believers of the Oneness, a Pentecostalist offshoot, was attending the burial of one of their own. Twelve of the faithful tended to Andrew Whitman, dead from a tooth infection that had traveled to his brain. The devout, some wailing, some rolling on the ground, some shaking in spasms as they spoke in tongues, and still others crying out in hysterics, beating their faces and chests with their hands, made their goodbyes, and many prayers to Jehovah to care for their loved one.

The head of the clan, Reverend Bishop, knelt with both hands raised to the heavens; in his left hand, he clutched a small Bible tightly, his body shaking violently from head to toe. He extorted loudly, "In the name of the Holy Spirit, I beg of you, dear Lord, to please… To Please… To *PLEASE!* have mercy on the soul of this man!" Wails of grief and overwrought sobs followed in earnest.

And on and on in this vain went the Pentecostalist committal service. When the service concluded, Horace, watching calmly from the sidelines, stepped over to the graveside to lower the casket into the ground. The congregation, their exhortations complete, were weeping softly as they slowly walked back to the patio of Horace's mortuary home to have a short post-burial reception.

HORACE, who was taking a break under the shade of a giant oak tree, waited patiently for Reverend Bishop's congregation to finish the reception. Horace had one more task to complete on this day before he could retire for the evening. As he rested, he replayed in his mind an incident that had occurred earlier that day during the showing of Gloria O'Neil.

Gloria's relations lined up to take their turn to say their last goodbyes to Gloria, who was lying in repose in her open casket. Horace noticed that several of those who had stepped near Gloria had made a face, inched their noses closer to Gloria, and then sniffed. He noted that some in the room had covered their noses with their handkerchiefs after finishing their turn at her casket.

Not long after, Gloria's husband, Francis O'Neil, approached Horace discretely, brought his face close to Horace's ear, cupped his hand to cover his mouth, and whispered, "I believe Gloria has turned a wee bit faster than expected... We might want to wrap this up an' get her in the ground—the sooner the better..."

After the guests shuffled out of the viewing room to wait outside for Gloria's casket to be rolled to her final resting spot, Horace discreetly walked over to Gloria, leaned in, and sniffed. *I smell nothing—I believe I did her embalming proper like "Not sure what all that hubbub was about,* he thought as he closed the lid shut and nailed it in place.

HAD Horace been of normal mind, he would have understood that Patty, Rose, Evelyn, and Frank we're not anything like the animated, happy friends that he imagined them to be. If he were able to see them as they *actually* were, rather than the visages that he wished upon them, he would have noticed that they were increasingly skeletal in appearance. Over time, the skin on their faces had receded, their lips shrinking back to the gum lines and exposing their teeth.

Evelyn's hair was coming out in clumps. Rose's face had lately developed a green patina of mold around her mouth and chin. Patty, the oldest of the mummies, had cracks in her skin along the line separating her leg from her torso, where Horace had repeatedly bent her legs from standing to sitting and back.

Evelyn's left eye had sunk inward after Horace, dancing the waltz with her, had dropped her on her face, smashing the orbital bone that held her eye in place.

All, in fact, had begun some degree of decomposition.

Had Horace been in a rational state of mind, he would have understood that this was where the rot that Gloria's guests had smelled had come from.

But Horace was not in *that* reality.

AFTER THE CONGREGATION finished the reception and had gone home, having had his rest under the oak tree, Horace started towards Mr. Whitman's grave. His final task of the day was to fill the grave with dirt and firmly pack it down. He whistled tonelessly to himself as he pumped the shovel loads into the hole, making hollow *thump* sounds as the dirt hit the coffin lid.

WHILE HORACE WAS out on the mortuary grounds, Mr. Méchant paid a visit to the mummies in the living room.

He entered the room suddenly from the side door, without notice or fanfare. He walked quietly to position himself in the middle of the room, facing the couch.

Mr. Méchant, standing before the four mummies, looked slowly from one to the other. Their souls, locked in their dead, desiccated bodies, stared back in fear at the dreadful demon before them.

Patty, in particular, having remembered Mr. Méchant's dire predictions of what was to become of her, quaked in her hooves at the reappearance of him.

"Ye need not be afraid of me," began Mr. Méchant in his deep voice, "You are not responsible for the fate that ye have found yourselves in. I am here to help you with your predicament. Please, if you will all be so kind as to follow my lead..."

With that, Mr. Méchant raised both his arms up at an elevated position, as if he were a conductor signaling his orchestra that the musical performance was about to begin. Immediately, the mummies snapped to attention, standing up directly from where they sat on the couch. Patty dropped from her seat onto all fours.

Not making a sound, the four looked directly into the red eyes of Mr. Méchant, mesmerized, as if standing at attention, like soldiers facing a General.

He then began to orchestrate, moving his hands up and down, right to left in circles and swirls; the mummies in turn circled and swirled, pivoted and pirouetted in dance, while they silently moved in figure eights about the living room. Patty hopped and pranced around their spinning feet. All the while, a smoke, sparkling and glittering with flashes of color, exuded from Mr. Méchant's fingers; the smoke dove, swirled, floated across the room, went into the eyes of each of them, filling their bodies with dark and fluid magic.

Mr. Méchant continued with this for five minutes more, and then just as suddenly as it had begun, he put his arms back at their upright positions. The mummies stopped in unison and stood rigidly at attention. He motioned with a single finger, and they all quickly returned to stand erect in front of their respective assigned places on the couch. He dropped his arms to his side. At once, the mummies sat back down into their original positions on the couch, all eyes focused on Mr. Méchant.

"I bid you goodnight," he said to his audience.

Then, just as abruptly as he had appeared, he walked out of the room and was gone.

"What just happened to us?" asked Frank to the others.

"I am not exactly sure, but I feel… different..." replied Rose, mystified.

They all nodded in agreement. They were indeed different, and they all suspected what *exactly* that difference was.

It was then that they began to discuss their predicament and what was to be done about it.

HORACE FINISHED PATTING the last of the dirt down onto Mr. Whitman's grave. He then headed back to the house to clean up and have some supper.

After he finished his meal, he headed into the living room to enjoy the warmth of camaraderie and *maybe a little something extra with Evelyn,* he thought with more than a smidgen of anticipation and excitement.

He stepped into the living room, walked across the wood floor, and plopped himself down in his rocker as he had done a hundred times before.

"How was everyone's day today? Mine be busier than a one-eyed cat watchin' nine rat holes," Horace said with a chuckle.

No one replied.

Startled by the silence, he looked from Patty to Rose to Evelyn to Frank.

He realized with a bolt of *What in Heaven's name?* running down his spine, they were looking at him silently. And not with friendly faces either, but with looks of anger, eyebrows angled down with indignant and white-hot hate written all over their expression.

Horace only managed, "Wha... Wha... Wha..." before spitting out: "What's gotten into y'all?"

"Why did you do this to me?" It was Patty who spoke first.

"I was happy in my pen... I could play with the other pigs. Play with you when you come to visit. But now, I am this... This... This... Thing!" Patty cried out.

"I was okay at first, I suppose; I didn't think much about the situation. But then you brought in Evelyn, and I realized then how it is that you just wanted me for your disgusting and perverted carnal acts," added Rose.

"And I was at peace with my death when it happened. But what am I now? I am not dead... I am not alive... What am I? Am I nothing more than a sex slave for your entertainment?" chimed in Evelyn, her eyes drilling into Horace with malice.

Frank stood up from his place on the couch and walked to Horace. He bent down to square his face with Horace's. "How do you justify taking my wife from her grave, making her into that *thing* you see sitting over there on your couch? How do you justify cracking my skull open with a hammer and then turning *me* into *this undead creature* that is doomed to sit on your couch and yammer at you as if *I LIKE YOU?*" yelled Frank into Horace's face.

Horace stood suddenly and looked at them all in confusion.

"You didn't answer me!" yelled Patty.

Patty jumped off the couch and hopped across the room to Horace. She stood upright on her hind legs and placed her front hooves on Horace's chest. She looked directly at him with anger flaring in her eyes. With reproach in her voice, she repeated her question: "Why did you do this to me?"

Her eyes demanded a response.

Mortification rooted Horace to the spot. Somewhere deep in Horace's insanity, he had always known his little "family" animation was only in his own mind. But this was different and highly disturbing. Had Horace been sane, however, he would have fully understood the gravity of the situation. He would have understood that Patty's hopping and talking, indeed the emotions, voices, and actions of all the mummies he had created, no longer had anything to do with him. They became animated of their own accord. They could do whatever they wanted.

Now and forever more.

But instead, Horace thought that he must be coming down with something, and he was hallucinating. The smoked pig meat he had eaten for supper had gone bad. Or one of the guests he had entertained graveside that day had passed some illness to him that had rendered him temporarily insane. Horace felt his forehead for evidence of the heat of fever. Unfortunately for Horace, his forehead was cool.

Horace broke his paralysis. He felt bewildered beyond reason and wanted nothing more but to leave this room. *I need to go to bed, that's what I need. A good night's sleep an' all this be gone…*

Horace slowly moved Patty's front paws off his chest, gently set her upright, and then placed her on the ground. He took one step towards the door. Frank stepped in front of him, blocking his path, and Horace found himself face-to-face with Frank yet again. Frank was breathing heavily. His puffs of stinking breath blew Horace's hair up from his scalp with each exhalation. Horace walked carefully around Frank, looked briefly at his glowering face, and ran from the room.

Horace ran all the way to his bedroom, not bothering to

take off his day clothes. He dove into his bed put his head under his blanket and pillow.

Horace did not sleep a wink that night. He had the horrifying idea that if he peeked out from under his pillow, he would see in the dark of his bedroom two red eyes staring down at him.

So, he didn't look.

VIII
THE END IS NIGH

When the rays of morning were just reaching the edge of the sky above his home, Horace was snoring a fitful, shallow sleep.

As the sunshine lit his eyelids, he popped awake with a snort. He had fallen asleep only a few short hours before dawn, and his eyes now felt full of sand.

He rose from his bed and looked at the small mirror he hung from the wall above the desk he used as his private office. The face that looked back at him was puffy. His eyes were red with fatigue from the weeping he had done during the quiet of the night, and his thoughts kept drifting back to the events of the previous evening. Horace never felt more alone or more afraid than he had this night.

Horace tiptoed to his dresser. He opened the top drawer as silently as he could, pulled out a leather strap he used as a belt, then tiptoed to the kitchen. When he reached the door leading to the living room, *thank God I thought of slamming the door shut when I ran out last night!* He thought as he tied the end of the strap around the door handle as quietly as possible. He then tied the other end of the strap to the heavy kitchen cabinet standing just to the right of the door. When finished and the door firmly tied shut, Horace let out an audible sigh of relief.

Just then, the protests from inside the living room erupted.

Horace heard loud footfalls as Frank ran to the door, trying to yank it open. The door slammed inward several times, stretching the leather strap tight with each strong pull, but the door held firm.

"Horace! You open this door at once!" yelled Frank.

Bang! Bang! Bang! Frank's fist smashed hard against the solid wood of the door.

Horace jumped backward at each bang on the door.

Horace turned and walked quickly out of the kitchen and away from the living room.

A FEW DAYS had passed in which, on each of these days, Horace would quietly slink past the living room from his bedroom, through the kitchen, and to the mortuary preparation room. There were more instances of banging and yelling from the other side of the living room door, but after two days of ignoring the protests, the clamor eventually abated. Horace could still make out the mumbling and burbling of conversations as the mummies talked amongst one another, but Horace did not want to ignite another round of caterwaul by signaling to them that he was nearby.

On the morning of the fourth day after the rebellion had begun, as Horace was on his way to the kitchen for his breakfast of hardtack and headcheese, he heard Rose address him through the living room door.

"Horace, we would like to talk with you, please," Rose said in a calm voice.

Horace stopped in his tracks, cocked his head towards the door to listen for signs of movement. He suspected a trap.

"Horace, please, darling, no tricks from us. We have

regained our composure. We just want to talk, that's all," said Rose. "Please, just open the door."

Horace, who had been confused, lonely, and hurt by these events, was suspicious. But, because of his love for Rose, he relented. He walked to the door and untied the strap from around the door handle. He put his arms to his side and expelled a long sigh as he waited.

The door creaked slowly open. On the other side, looking back at Horace was Rose. Although her face was serious and stern, she did not appear angry. *Or about to leap on me and beat me about the face like that other night,* thought Horace.

"Come in, Horace. Please, sit yourself at your customary place." Rose gestured with her hand to the rocker.

Horace quickly looked from Rose to Evelyn, then to Frank, and finally to Patty. Their faces wore no warm greetings, but the mad anger was gone. He felt uneasy at their cool demeanor, but despite this, he trudged across the room, head and shoulders slumped, and sank heavily into his rocker. He kept his head down, looking only at his feet. *I feel like a child about to be scolded,* he thought.

Frank began.

"We need to figure out a way out of this mess, Horace. You *do* realize that this... this... situation we find ourselves in is not natural?" Frank paused to give Horace a chance to respond; when Horace only sat staring at his hands, he continued: "We want you to do something to reverse things. Whatever it was you did to us, make it go away. We don't want to be these... these... *things* anymore."

"And I want a divorce," Rose chimed in emphatically.

"Me too. A divorce," added Evelyn, her head nodding up and down in an equally assertive manner as Rose.

"And I don't want to play with you anymore," called out Patty, her two front hooves crossed defiantly on her chest.

Once again, Horace found himself looking from face to face and back again. Then suddenly, as if their words came crashing down onto his shoulders, weighing him down, he buried his head into his hands and sobbed. Deep, wrenching sobs.

"Reverse it? Reverse it? I don't know how!" cried Horace in a half-sob, half-willful tone.

He continued, "Why are you doing this to me? Rose? *A divorce?* I love you. How am I going to live without you?"

The last "you" came out as a blubbering "y-y-y-oooooouuu…!" ending with more uncontrolled sobbing.

"I am truly sorry you feel pain, Horace, but do you really love me? Do you? How can you possibly understand our pain? Or should I say, 'lack of it' because we are undead," came Evelyn, no small amount of malice in her voice.

Seeing the anger rising in them and fearing it would spiral out of control, Horace sprinted from the room, slamming the living room door behind him—though forgetting to tie it shut —and ran into the safety of the mortuary preparation room.

HORACE WAS SITTING at his small workbench, turning the events of the day over in his mind while listening to the backdrop of discussion between the mummies in the living room, Horace cupped his hand to his ear, but the voices were too distant for him to make out what they were saying. Suddenly, the murmuring from the living room ceased, and all was quiet—a moment later, the squeak of an un-oiled wagon wheel drifted in from the front yard.

People were approaching the house. Horace jumped from his chair, ran through the entry door, and walked quickly out onto the mortuary entryway to greet the visitors.

Two Maury County Sheriffs pulled the wagon. In the wagon lay two bodies. One was that of a man, in his forties by appearance, the entire top of his head missing. The other was of a young woman, *almost, but not quite marrying age, based on her appearance,* thought Horace; her neck bruised by what looked like large hand marks.

When the men with the wagon in tow reached Horace, they stopped to introduce themselves.

"I am Sheriff Jacob Hasseling, and this is my partner, Sheriff John McDonald," said the taller of the two.

"Pleased to make your acquaintance. How can I be of service to y'all on this day?" Horace replied as he looked at the two dead bodies draped across the wagon bed.

"These two are about as sorry a story as it gets," began Sheriff Hasseling, "The man lying there is Mr. Lemenski," pointing to the man draped in the wagon, "... and this be his daughter Doris," pointing to the dead young woman next to him.

"What happened?" asked Horace, continuing to look at the bodies.

"Mr. Lemenski had a propensity with drinkin' and when he tips back a bit too much, why he takes to beating his wife. A month back, she got fed up with his nonsense, an' she up an' left his sorry ass," explained Sheriff McDonald.

"Not too long after she left 'im, he got to chasing after his daughter Doris there for the unnatural act that God forbid between a father and daughter," Sheriff McDonald said, pointing to the dead girl.

"Doris threatened to tell of the unnatural acts her father was forcing on her, so he strangled her when she tried to leave," broke in Sheriff Hasseling, "I'm a-guessin' the shame be too much at what he done for he took his shotgun an' blew his own fool head off."

"Sad story it is," finished Sheriff McDonald. Both Sheriff McDonald and Sheriff Hasseling looked down at their hands as they shook their heads show how pathetic the situation was.

"How do y'all want me to be disposing of these two?" asked Horace.

"Burn 'em," came their dry reply, "No relative wants 'em. The wife be gone for good. No need for a coffin or service. The sheriff's office will pay the customary rate for the cremation, of course."

After a brief discussion, and once everyone had agreed on the price, the two sheriff deputies said their goodbyes and left, leaving the wagon with Doris and Mr. Lemenski still inside.

They gave Horace the instruction to return the wagon when he completed his task.

Horace grabbed Doris by the arm, dragging her into the mortuary preparation room, then dumping her onto the floor, her head making a loud *thunk* as it landed hard on the ground. He then returned once more to the wagon to grab Mr. Lemenski. He dragged him out back to the crematorium.

Horace dumped Mr. Lemenski onto the cold ground unceremoniously, the gore that remained of his head making a wet *splat* as it flopped to the dirt. He planned to cremate Mr. Lemenski first.

Horace was about to open the crematorium door to throw Mr. Lemenski in, when the germ of an idea popped into his head: *Kill two birds with one stone, I will!* He left Mr. Lemenski where he lay and returned to the mortuary preparation room. Once there, he pulled Doris up and onto the embalming table. He stepped back to look at her. *She be a pretty, young thing,* came his thoughts, *I do not need those in there,* glancing at the living room door—*they be poisoned. A divorce! Rose wants a divorce, does she? Well, I have a response to her, I'll divorce her! I divorce them all! This one here, be my new bride. All those in the living room—those be traitors. I'll burn 'em up with that Mr. Lemenski!*

At that, Horace smiled.

It was then that Horace came upon another idea… He had never had a woman who was not "prepared" as Rose and

Evelyn were. *Mayhap that makes a difference... Mayhap it feel better if'n their flesh be fresh...*

It did not take long for Horace to pull the clothing from Doris and begin the act.

I be correct in my figurin'—he thought to himself as he lay on top of her—*it does feel a lot better when they're fresh!*

FRANK, Rose, Evelyn, and Patty were sitting on the couch in the living room discussing their situation when Doris, or more accurately, the ghost of Doris, broke into the living room in a state of panic.

"He's doing the 'unnatural' thing to my body! Just like my Daddy did to me when I was alive! Make him stop! Please make him stop!" screamed the ghost of Doris as she ran in circles, her hands clamped tight to the crown of her head,

"Oh, this cannot stand!" cried Frank, "Forget trying to make peace with that monster, we must do something, and do it now."

Rose, Evelyn, and Patty nodded in agreement.

Doris stopped her hysterics, pleading, "Oh. Thank you. Thank you. How can I help?"

Rose looked at Doris and said, "Follow our lead..."

And Doris did.

They stood in unison, stepped to the door, slammed it open, and walked into the mortuary preparation room.

Horace, still mounted on top of Doris, looked back at them in surprise.

"Whaaaaa???" was all Horace could manage before he pulled out and yanked his pants up.

"Horace! You will pay for your crimes against Nature and God before this night is over!" yelled Frank.

Horace, seeing the rage, anger, and most of all, hunger for

revenge on all their faces, ran in terror from the room and out the back.

"HE'S HEADING out to the pig pen!" yelled Frank as he watched Horace run down the path, "You two: Rose an' Patty, head down the dirt road to the back of the pig pen and come up from behind. Myself an' Evelyn will come along the back path an' trap him there! Doris: You follow Horace—keep us informed where he is heading."

Before leaving, Rose and Evelyn each grabbed a sharp butchering knife from the worktable. Frank grabbed the sledgehammer. He flipped it in his hand a couple of times, smiled an evil smile, and said in a soft, deep growl: "I am so looking forward to seein' this in the back of that evil little man's head."

"I have a better end for our dear Horace… call it poetic justice," said Rose to Frank.

Frank's evil smile grew even wider, as he knew exactly what she had in mind—they all nodded in silent agreement. With that, they quickly pulled out what they needed from Horace's supply cabinet.

They worked quickly and completed the necessary preparations in minutes, after which, they followed Frank out of the mortuary, building at a fast pace, leaving Doris's body to lie on the table. On her way out the door, the disembodied spirit of Doris looked back at her dead body and said to it, "So sad this day has been… I will get you your revenge, my dear Doris." She blew herself a final kiss, then turned and ran down the trail.

HORACE HAD FLED to the far end of the pig pen. Just across the road from where he stood was the hay field from which he had first encountered Mr. Méchant. A shiver ran through him as he looked back to that day—before any of this mess had begun. He suspected a connection between the man and the events that followed, but he didn't know what. Horace was confused and desperate to find a way out of his situation.

How can it be that my friends have turned on me so suddenly? How did this come to be? His frustrated thoughts echoed in his mind as he paced up and down the trail. *What to do?* Back and forth with nervous frustration, he walked. *What to do?* So deep in his own thoughts he failed to notice that all his pigs were inside their shelters, cowering in fear from what was coming down the trail toward him.

Horace had turned to pace once more when Rose stepped from around the corner. She had a look on her face that screamed hate, with a generous helping of revenge. She tilted her face downward, but her eyes, unblinking, looked directly into his, drilling into him. A chill of fresh terror ran down his spine when he saw the knife pointed directly at the soft of his belly.

"Rose, please… put the knife down… let's talk," said Horace, his voice quaking with fear.

"I will put it down, my Dear Horace, when you are dead," she replied, her voice icy.

Horace was about to dart around Rose to make his escape when Evelyn stepped out from her hiding place behind the pig pen and quickly took up position to the right of Rose, blocking him. Evelyn held her knife out in the same menacing manner as Rose. Horace could only back out and shy away from them. He did this slowly, stepping backward one step, then two, then three. He spun around, intending to run east, but just as suddenly, Frank and Patty stepped out from the east trail, blocking that route of escape.

Rose, Evelyn, Frank, and Patty stepped closer to box him in.

Patty snapped her jaw *Snap! Snap!* lunging forward with each chomp. Horace pressed himself back into the fencing of the pig pen to escape her.

"Please Patty, stop!" cried Horace.

"Maybe I bite off your little cock, you bastard!" yelled Patty back as she snapped her jaw again, this time close to his crotch. Horace screamed in terror and tried to dance away, grabbing his neither region with both hands to protect his manhood, only to crash into the fence. Patty snorted and laughed in glee at his discomfort.

"We will be free of you now, you horrible little monster of a man!" yelled Frank.

It was at that moment the sight of the little girl wearing a formal dress and shiny patent leather shoes standing on the grass not far from him distracted Horace . *What in the name of God is a little girl doing in the graveyard at this hour?* was all Horace managed to think before they made their move.

Horace's distraction was enough for Frank to quickly grab both his arms while Rose tied them with the very same strap Horace had used to trap them in their living room. With Horace secure, Frank hoisted him up and over his shoulders —surprising Horace with his strength.

"I demand you let me down! Where are you taking me?," pleading Horace, his voice shaking at each bounce of Frank's steps down the trail.

"I'll not put you down. I aim to put an end to this for good," replied Frank, his voice firm and determined.

As Frank carried him away, Horace spied the little girl still standing where he had first seen her. She waved goodbye to him, then quickly turned, and walked away without a look back. Horace never saw her again.

THE GROUP REACHED THE CREMATORIUM. As Frank continued to hold Horace foisted onto his shoulder, Evelyn opened the oven door. Horace watched helplessly in shock as Evelyn threw a large pile of eucalyptus leaves down onto the floor of the crematorium chamber.

"No! Please! What are you going to do?" cried Horace, a look of horror on his face.

"Only what you did to us," replied Rose. "Oh, we can't forget an important step, can we…" Rose ran into the preparation room a moment before returning with two containers. Horace watched as Rose soaked the leaves in cedar oil and sprinkled them generously with myrrh resin. "... now it will smoke nicely for hours."

Frank lowered Horace to the ground, ignoring his frantic pleading for his life.

While Frank held him tight, Rose cut Horace's clothing from his body using the knife she still held. Soon, he was naked. Embarrassed by his vulnerability, he instinctively tried to cover his privates, but could not escape Frank's strong grasp of his wrists.

"I wanted to split your head open with my sledgehammer, Horace, but Rose here had a better idea for your fate," said Frank.

Evelyn, standing nearby, held a gallon jar filled to the brim with pine tar distillate. She tipped the jar over Horace's head, the distillate spilling onto him, its sticky liquid forming an oil slick down his back, shoulders, and chest. Rivulets of which soaked the ground around him.

She then grabbed a cloth bag, and from it, threw handfuls of powder, a mixture of salt, sugar, and powdered cinnamon, at Horace, covering him head to toe. The salt stung Horace's eyes, blinding him.

When Rose finished, Frank lifted Horace over his head. Horace screamed, "No! Don't do this! Please don't do this!

NO!" as Frank carried him over to the crematorium. When they reached the oven door, Frank threw Horace inside the chamber.

Before Horace could regain his balance, Evelyn slammed the door shut and locked it.

After a short pause, Horace pounded frantically on the door from the inside, a muffled "Let me out! Please! Please don't do this!"

Rose walked over to the gas valve, turned on the gas, lit the pilot, and turned the flames down low.

The mummies, in unison, walked away towards the back of the mortuary grounds.

Horace began to scream in pain as the flames lit the leaf pile and the smoke grew thick and hot.

His screams rang out all the way to the back of the graveyard, but the mummies paid it no mind. They smiled at each other. Patty leaped and pranced with joy.

"Soon, we will be free," said Frank.

A short time later, as they stood in a grass hollow near the northwestern corner of the memorial grounds, they heard the screams stop. They all knew at once that Horace was in his final throes and, in short order, would be dead.

Or undead, thought Frank.

The moment Horace's heart stopped beating, Frank, Rose, Evelyn, and Patty fell to the ground and lay still. Whatever life force Mr. Méchant had given them was gone. They were once again the helpless spirits trapped in the desiccated, hollowed-out remnants of their human bodies that they were before Mr. Méchant visited the living room.

As they lay in the grass, their view was of the blue sky above. Suddenly, a little girl's head, the same little girl who once visited them in the living room only to run away in fear, appeared in their frame of view and looked down at them. From Rose's vantage, the little girl was standing just above Rose's head and bent over to look down at her face. This time, the little girl did not appear to be afraid.

"Hello. My name is Francesca," she said calmly to Rose. Francesca turned her head to look at the other mummies to address them as well, "You needn't worry—Ariel will soon be here to help y'all!" she said excitedly, clapping her hands with glee.

Francesca stood up and stepped out of view. In her place, birds filled their sight—hundreds of them flitting in and out, excitedly chirp-chirping as they darted to and fro.

A raccoon came up to Rose and sniffed at her face before walking out of view. A dozen squirrels, their gray fluffy tails snapping up and down, jumped the gap in branches between the two trees overhead. Ladybugs, giant centipedes, and walking sticks walked up and over Rose's face. They were all heading in the same direction, somewhere just to the south of her feet.

What's going on, Frank? Rose thought in Frank's direction.

I don't know, but there's a gatherin' just over yonder... Frank thought back to Rose.

A few minutes later, the chirps, squeaks, click-clicks, the calls of animals and insects of all types, stopped in unison. There was only silence.

Then a flash of light lit the sky above them.

They heard footsteps approaching. Not the footsteps of a child but those of an adult.

Momentarily, the face of a beautiful woman appeared, looking down at them; the rays of the sun shining through her hair directly behind her head made it appear as if the woman wore a crown of golden sunlight.

"Hello everyone... My name is Ariel," said the woman,

introducing herself, "I see you met Francesca. Francesca has decided to join us today on our trip through the curtain.

"And now it is time for you to go into the beyond."

The mummies watched as the hand of Ariel floated into view. The hand that looked made to play violins, compose poetry, inspire children to sit quietly and listen, tame lions with gentle strokes to their manes, opened palm up.

"Up," said Ariel in a beautiful lilting voice at the same moment the index finger of her outstretched hand made a *Get Up! Get Up!* motion.

And lickety-split, the ghosts of Rose, Evelyn, and Frank stood upright. Patty, being a pig, stood on all fours. They now faced Ariel, all looking expectantly at her.

"Follow me," said Ariel, her voice soft and pleasant.

They followed in single-line formation; Rose first, followed by Evelyn, then by Frank, and finally Patty, as she led them to the curtain. It surprised Rose to see the mesh of interlocking insects that created the curtain. When Ariel reached the curtain, Francesca, with the ghost of Doris next to her, walked up to Ariel and each took Ariel by a hand. Together, Ariel, Doris, and Francesca walked into the gap in the parted curtain.

And as they silently stepped through together, Francesca took one look back over her shoulder at the graveyard that had been her home for these long seventy years. She whispered "goodbye" as they disappeared into the place beyond.

At the moment she disappeared, a flash of light lit the grounds around them, Francesca had finally joined her mother. Rose, Evelyn, Frank, and Patty, each in turn, followed through the curtain and into the beyond.

They were gone.

The remains of the mummies lay on the grass; the empty shells that they now were would remain where they had fallen forever. Ariel saw to it that the insects would reduce their flesh to pulp and their bone to dust. Grass would grow over to disguise their bodies. Wildflowers would become their blankets. In the years to follow, a person who happened to walk past this patch of ground would only see gentle bumps in the ground, completely unaware of what those bumps once were.

The fate of Horace, however, was a different story.

IX
OFF STAGED BY SHEPHERD'S CROOK

The morning of the third day following Horace's living cremation, a hand with unnaturally long fingers and long, long fingernails reached for the crematorium door. The fingers wrapped around the door handle and rotated the handle to the left before pulling. The door swung wide open. Collapsed at the back of the chamber was a very dead, very desiccated Horace. His leathery skin tanned from the spices and smoke. His eyes, still open but shriveled, were smoky gray. His mouth was open in a grimace, his final scream frozen on his face, forever.

Although Horace was dead, his ghost remained in the shell of his body. He was unable to escape it and thus lay helpless as he looked out the crematorium door and at the frightful face of a man who looked in upon him. He recognized him as the man he had seen across the way those many months ago. Horace thought, *Not a man, but a demon.* The demon smiled at Horace with cruel delight. The red flames in his eyes were particularly hot and bright at this moment.

"We have not been properly introduced, my dear Mr. Horace Graves... "I am Mr. Méchant," said the demon, placing his hand on his chest and bowing slightly in mock formal introduction.

"You will now sit with me in your living room, Horace. But it is not proper for ye to be naked now, is it? Hum? First, you must be dressed properly... don't you think?" Not waiting for a reply from the ghost of Horace, Mr. Méchant growled as he reached in to grab him, pulling him from the corner of the chamber, and lifted him out and onto his shoulders.

Horace could only watch with horror from within the prison of his mummified body as Mr. Méchant carried him into the house, past the body of Doris, now green with decay as she lay where Horace left her. Mr. Méchant sat Horace on a kitchen chair next to Doris, her left leg just touching Horace's shoulder. Despite all that Horace had done and seen, he shivered inside his dead body at the thought of touching the green, decomposing leg of Doris.

Just to taunt him, Mr. Méchant grabbed the left hand of Doris and pantomimed her jacking off Horace's shriveled, desiccated penis.

"Ha! Ha! Ha! Ha!" howled Mr. Méchant, "Not as nice as when Rose did this I see! Hum?" as he dropped Doris's hand, "Or more accurately, when you grabbed Rose's mummified hand and used it to masturbate yourself with. Is that not correct, Horace?

"You know that Rose's palm be worn to the bone from your constant need for self-abuse, don't you?"

Horace's ghost cringed with revulsion.

Mr. Méchant walked to Horace's bedroom. Horace could hear him open dresser drawers and open closet doors. In a few moments, Mr. Méchant returned with what Horace recognized as his best suit. Mr. Méchant worked purposefully for the next half hour, first heating an iron on the stove, then meticulously ironing the items Horace was to wear. When finished, he fitted Horace with the newly ironed undergarments, socks, pants, belt, shirt, jacket, hat, and finally, tie. After buttoning the top button of Horace's shirt, Mr. Méchant carefully tied his tie in a Four-in-Hand knot, cinching the knot tight around his neck like a noose.

Finished, Mr. Méchant clamped his hands around Horace's shoulders, and looking into Horace's face, said: "Now ye be a proper, *dapper* mortician!"

At that, Mr. Méchant slapped his knee and belted out a loud guffaw.

"Into the living room, ye go!"

Mr. Méchant picked Horace up, carried him to the living room, and lowered him onto the rocker. Mr. Méchant then sat himself down at Evelyn's spot on the couch next to Horace, flopping himself down into the cushion of the couch in an exaggerated manner, as if to say, "Ahhhhh! Now this is comfortable!"

"Rose no longer needs this seat now, does she?" mocked Mr. Méchant.

"Unlike your pathetic self, s*he* has gone behind the curtain and into the light beyond," said Mr. Méchant with a deep and menacing chuckle.

If Horace could have responded, he would have begged Mr. Méchant for mercy. Mercy to end whatever it was that Mr. Méchant had in store for him.

"Now this room is all yours. You have all the time in the world to think of the choices ye have made for yourself; the things ye have done here.

"From time to time, I will come back to visit.

"Until then, my Dear Horace, I will be on my way.

"I bid ye adieu."

With that, Mr. Méchant rose from the couch and walked from the living room.

Horace was utterly alone.

A tear, one lonely teardrop, formed in the fold of Horace's right eye and dripped down his dry, mummified face. It fell from his chin to his lap.

FORTY YEARS HAD PASSED. The trees of the mortuary had grown taller by several dozen feet. The shrubs, weeds, and grass, untended all this time, had filled the cemetery up, until, if one were to have passed along the road and looked out onto these grounds, one would have seen only open space, a wild patch of the forest, the gravestones completely obscured from view by the growth. The roof of Horace's home, rotted from years of weather and rain, had fallen in.

Coyotes and foxes scouring the kitchen for scraps had scattered Doris's bones.

The old oak tree at the back of the cemetery that suffered a lightning bolt a dozen years ago now lay on its side, crushing a cluster of headstones that had the misfortune of being in its path.

Although the mummification process drastically slowed the decomposition process, time had taken a toll on Horace's body. Mold slowly ate away at his fingers and toes, exposing bone at their tips. His nose had fallen off and now rested in his lap. His eyeballs had shriveled and dried, collapsing inward, leaving his eye sockets empty. The skin of his face had dried and shriveled around his eye sockets and mouth, giving his face a look that was closer to a skull than a human face.

Since no one removed his internal organs before placing him in the crematorium oven, enough moisture remained for anaerobic bacteria to slowly consume them, despite the body being thoroughly dried.

Every week or so, the pressure would build to the point of rapid release, and Horace would belch an awful stench of green gas. Had any humans entered the living room, the strong smell of sewer gas would have overwhelmed them.

The road out front, Franklin Pike, was but a dirt path

when Horace was still alive. In the years since, the road was, first, graveled, then later paved.

A large Keep Out! Private Property! sign, installed at the arrangement of Mr. Méchant shortly after Horace's mummification (he had the power to appear in the physical world as an ordinary man if he so chose), having been installed by a chain across the entryway to the property, now lay on the ground; the chain having broken in a particularly violent storm. The sign lay rusted and covered in leaves.

It did not matter that the keep out sign lay out of sight, the occasional passerby, in the initial few years by horse-drawn wagon, but in the latter years by automobile, did not bother to stop, or even look at the wreckage of the mortuary grounds. They were far too busy heading either north to Nashville, where the action was, or south to Columbia, to worry about the sodden breakdown carnage of the house still visible through the overgrowth.

During a powerful spring windstorm, a tree limb—about as thick as a large man's upper leg—broke free from the tree and crashed through the living room wall. From where Horace sat, he could look out through the hole it had made and onto the green of the yard beyond. This gave Horace little pleasure, though, as the tedium of his isolation was crushing.

Every so often, Horace would spy a man looking in at him through the hole. The ghost of Horace would call out to the man in his thoughts: *Hey, Mister! Would you come in for a visit? Please? I sure could use some company...* But the man would stare at him for a moment or two and walk on his way. Horace had never formally met Mr. Buchanan and had no way of knowing that Mr. Buchanan was himself a ghost and thus could hear his pleading; but, had Mr. Buchanan had the chance, he would have explained to Horace that Mr. Méchant had expressly forbidden him to get too near to Horace, or to engage with him in any way whatsoever—and Mr. Buchanan had no intention of disobeying Mr. Méchant. *No Sir!*

Other than the occasional appearance of Mr. Buchanan's ghost, no one, not human, not a coyote, not fox, nor squirrel, or raven, not even a rat for that matter, paid a visit to Horace. Mr. Méchant saw to that. Horace was to remain utterly alone. Except for his own rare visits that was.

One day, a twelve-year-old boy named Abraham wandered onto the mortuary grounds while hunting rabbits. He was walking among the gravestones, looking for rabbit trails he could follow, when a man suddenly walked up to him from his right. Abraham assumed the man was Mr. Graves, the property owner, although this was surprising to Abraham, as he had heard that no one had seen Mr. Graves in years.

The man introduced himself, "Hello, young man, my name is Mr. Buchanan, and I am afraid you are on private property. I beg of you to leave this place."

Abraham, raised in a strict Reformist Christian faith, replied politely, "I'm sorry, Mister, I didn't mean no harm—jus' huntin' rabbit is all," as he raised his rifle to show as proof.

"That is fine, my young fellow, I not be angry; but you must leave now," this he said as he made shooing gestures towards the property line.

Abraham dutifully turned and walked towards where he had entered the property. After a few paces, he turned around to look back at Mr. Buchanan. Mr. Buchanan had himself turned to walk back to his grave, the bloody hatchet wound in the back of his head now clearly visible to Abraham. Abraham screamed bloody murder, peed in his pants, and ran for his life, never to return.

Every few years, Mr. Méchant would visit Horace, still sitting on his rocker in the living room of his house, everything in the house rotting around him. Tendrils of ivy grew along the walls and hung from the busted-in roof line. Dribbles of rain dripped onto the couch, rotting it clean through. Rusted couch springs were all that remained of most of it.

"How are you doing my dear Horace? Is it quiet enough for ye?" mocked Mr. Méchant. A deep and evil belly laugh always followed. The red of his eyes would flare in brilliant flames to match the intensity of his laugh.

"Don't ye worry none, soon this place will be sold; and after that, I will come to call ye home with me," an evil smile spread on Mr. Méchant's face, "I will then be entertained by your screams as ye dance in my lake of fire."

Horace could only scream silently, in the small space that remained of his mind, having gone mad from the torment of his long isolation.

It was now the early 1960s, and investors were investing, builders were building, and homebuyers were purchasing homes in and around Springdale. Soon, Mr. Mechant—the sole beneficiary of Horace Graves's estate—sold the property. Mr. Mechant also arranged for Horace Graves to be declared dead in absentia.

As the final *coup d'état,* Mr. Méchant would also see to the sale of the property.

Mr. Méchant laughed a deep, resonant belly laugh all the way out the door as he left Horace for this one last time.

Soon, it would be time to call Horace home.

The End

ABOUT THE AUTHOR

John is a retired pharmaceutical biochemist and software engineer currently living in a rural section of

Tennessee. His previous residence of thirty-three years was that of the San Francisco Bay Area. He lives in a wonderful home with his wife situated on a few acres of wooded property where he tends to a large garden, and to his flock of chickens. His hobbies include do-it-yourself electronics projects, attending music festivals, visiting his greater family in California and Colorado, and, of course, fiction writing.

John's writing spans the spectrum between science fiction

and horror, wherever his fruitful and nightmarish imagination takes him.

His stories can be found in various anthologies and e-Zines by Terror Tract Publishing LLC, Hellbound Books Publishing LLC, Wicked Shadow, and Dragon Soul Press.

ALSO BY NIGHTMARE PRESS!!

The Guardians
Teresa Sewell and Rob Le

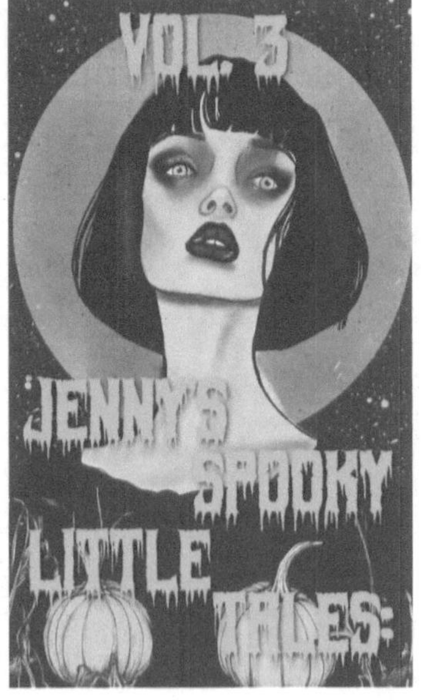
VOL. 3
JENNY'S
SPOOKY
LITTLE
TALES:

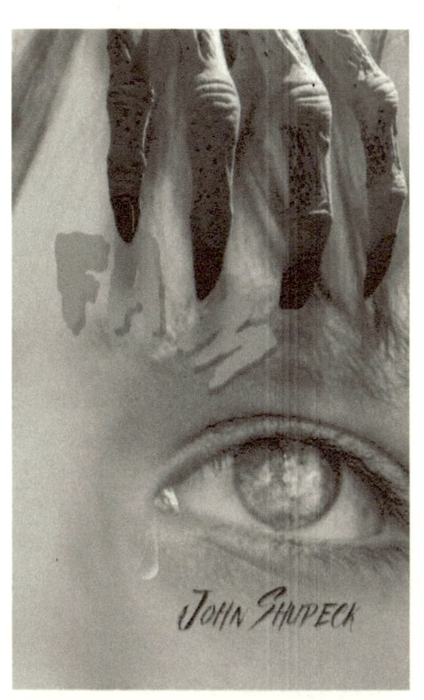
JOHN SHUPECK

WHITE TRASH
SUBLIME

COMING SOON FROM NIGHTMARE PRESS

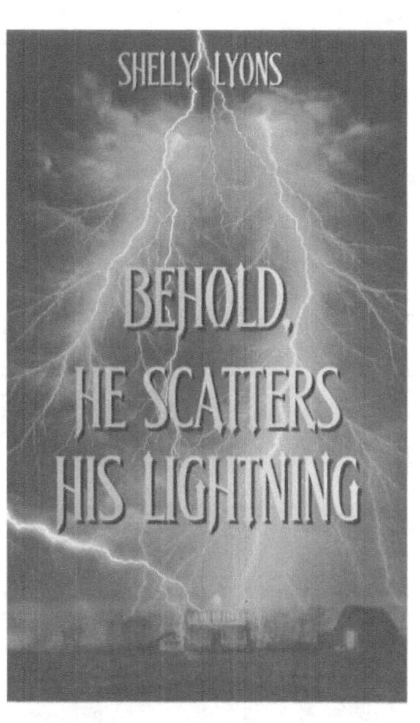

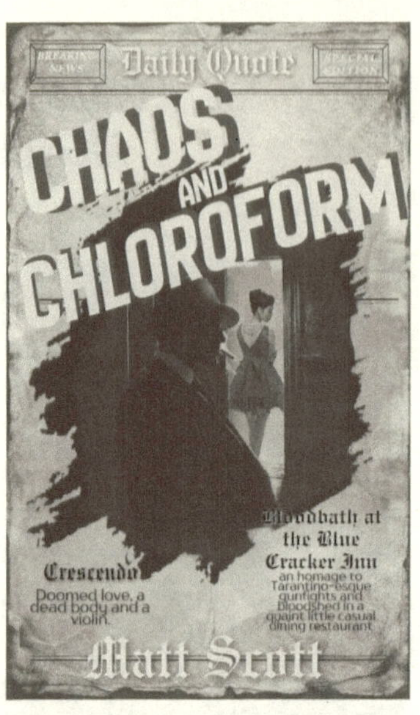
Daily Quote
CHAOS
AND
CHLOROFORM
Crescendo
Doomed love, a dead body and a violin.
Bloodbath at the Blue Cracker Inn
an homage to Tarantino-esque gunfights and bloodshed in a quaint little casual dining restaurant
Matt Scott

MAMA
JOSIE
G.E. MOORE

JOSEPH J. BATTAGLIA
THE
CONTINUANCE

SNARE FOR A SMALL
ECLIPSE
JASON A. WYCKOFF

SPOOKHOUSE

SHELDON WOODBURY

www.ingramcontent.com/pod-product-compliance
Lightning Source LLC
LaVergne TN
LVHW051009080826
845145LV00009B/2541

* 9 7 8 1 6 4 9 0 5 0 4 6 5 *